The Perfect Crime?

Winners of
The Guardian/Piccadilly
teenage writing competition

Piccadilly Press • London

Set in Justlefthand and Meridien

Printed and bound by Bookmarque Ltd
for the publishers Piccadilly Press Ltd,
5 Castle Road, London NW1 8PR

A catalogue record for this book is available
from the British Library

ISBN: 1 85340 791 7 (trade paperback)

1 3 5 7 9 10 8 6 4 2

Typeset by Textype Typesetters
Cover design by Judith Robertson

Contents

Foreword

There were three main reasons for my decision to stop writing fiction a few years back: age, lack of freshness, paucity of ideas. It was predictable, therefore, that I would feel envious of the entrants for this writing competition. They were all young – several of them very young. Most of the stories were fresh as the morning delivery of milk. And the majority were rich in originality of ideas. I found it difficult to decide on the gradations of merit, and several of the stories will ever remain in my mind.

It's a tricky business, this short story genre. Ideally, I think, such a story should germinate and blossom from a single idea – like a summer rose gradually blooming in its own right as it develops, oblivious to the dahlias and daisies around it. I never adequately mastered the skill myself. Almost all the short stories I wrote were long stories which I clipped and clipped until they became shorter and shorter. I could, therefore – and *did* – learn a good deal from this splendid selection of prize-winners.

Let me not be *over*-complimentary, however. As a whole, the *technical* presentation of stories fell somewhat short of their *imaginative* potential. There is no shortcut to the top of Olympus, and it behoves us all to respect – indeed to venerate – the niceties of our wonderful English language: spelling, construction of sentences, grammatical accuracy, and – above all! – punctuation.

Colin Dexter

Love Lessons

Katherine Davidson

Love Lessons

'By 1938 Hitler was in complete control of the whole of Germany and had established his power over the population. Anyone who dared to threaten his leadership was "disposed of" by the SS, or secret police . . .'

'Sounds a bit like your teaching policy, Sir. Anyone who doesn't agree with you gets chucked out. Isn't that right, Sir?'

'I can't really see a great deal of similarity between my classroom and 1940s Germany, Laura. Yes, I do "chuck out", as you so eloquently put it, anyone who disrupts my class, but I think it is a little extreme to compare it to the brutal murders committed by the SS.'

'Oh come on, Sir! We all know the only reason you bother with detentions is because Miss Baker won't let you install gas showers in the History class-rooms.'

James Welsh opened his mouth to give her a detention, hesitated, then closed it again, gaping like a goldfish in search of a retort.

'All hail Mr Welsh, Führer of class 11B!'

The bell rang with ironic good timing. The class saluted and marched out of the room, led, of course, by Laura Collins, who held a pencil stub between her nose and top lip to represent a moustache. James watched as the students left the room, carefully waiting until the door rattled shut behind the last girl, then let his head fall to the desk with a thump. He closed his eyes, wishing himself elsewhere, then ventured a glance and was almost surprised to find himself still in the classroom. Sighing in resignation, he picked up his disproportionately large pile of paperwork and sloped off to the staff room, ignoring the sheets that fluttered out of his files and fell to the corridor floor like paper footprints.

James lived in a one-bedroom flat on the outskirts of town. The rent was extortionate, but it was better than living with his mother. That night, as usual, he drove home in his battered Metro, listening to the monotonous buzzing of the radio – this was all he could hear since he bent the aerial driving under a low branch. He arrived at his flat, opened the car door and watched numbly as his paperwork slid out of the foot-well and clung to the grimy pavement. Scooping up as much as he could, he ran inside and climbed the three flights of stairs to his apartment. He closed the door behind him, flung his papers down and sank to the floor, cradling his face in his hands. It was days like this that made James wonder why he ever became a teacher.

Actually, he decided, it was pupils like Laura.

He made a ready meal and ate it out of the plastic carton while he did his marking. At midnight, he fell asleep over his lesson plan.

He was outside himself as he walked to the classroom. Laura was sitting on his desk, alone, chewing gum and winding it around her finger. As he entered, she smiled slyly and suddenly the classroom was full of people – the children, the head, his mother – all laughing and whispering to one another. He looked back at Laura. Her head was tipped back and he could see her uvula jiggle and squirm as she laughed. She surrounded him and her taunts echoed inside his skull and she swallowed him whole.

Tuesday. James woke, sitting up sharply, a timetable stuck to his sweaty cheek. He peeled it off gingerly and lurched over to the sink to splash water on his face. Then he poured himself a coffee with trembling hands.

Loaded with caffeine, he stood up and declared to the world and no one in particular that today he would beat Laura at her own game. However, this declaration was somewhat spoiled by the fact that immediately after he caught sight of the clock and swore to himself, rushed out of the flat, paused, and re-entered to pick up his car keys and folders.

James glanced at himself in the rear-view mirror

and smacked the dashboard when he realised what he looked like: stubble sprouting on his chin, yesterday's shirt and jacket, and cavernous shadows under his eyes. The traffic was abominable. It was raining and one of his windscreen wipers was broken. By the time James got to school the sun had come out, but gloom clung to him like the dampness in the air.

'All right, Sir? Slept in a dumpster again, Sir? They don't pay teachers enough these days, do they, Sir?'

Laura was sitting on his desk, her legs swinging back and forth. She was chewing, open-mouthed, and a breath of spearmint wafted across the room as she coiled a string of gum around her index finger. James started, thinking back to his dream.

'Laura, spit that out now!' She jumped off the desk and flounced across to the bin, sticking the lump to the inside of the lid for some unsuspecting cleaner to find. Then she sat down behind a desk and crossed her legs, pouting. 'And take that crap off your face.'

'Crap, Sir? That's not a very suitable word for class. And it's not crap, Sir, it's *"Bourgeois"*.'

'Is that a brand? It doesn't sound very, well, you, but I suppose there isn't a brand called "Cheap Tart".' James dropped his insult casually as he handed out a pile of worksheets. 'Whatever it is, take it off.'

'"Cheap Tart?" I happen to think it makes me look very attractive and sophisticated, don't you think,

Sir?' Laura flicked her hair over her shoulder and batted her eyelashes. James didn't even look at her. She sniffed. 'Well, at least I'm not wearing *"Eau de Hangover".'* The class sniggered.

'I can't see why it matters how you look anyway. It's an all-girls school. So . . . either you're hankering after me, or you're batting for the other side, shall we say.' He smirked as Laura blushed brighter than her pink powder.

'A lot of girls wear make-up to school,' she stuttered. 'And, just for the record, I am very much straight.'

'Oh, *very much* straight! That means you're – how would you say it? – loose? Comfortable with your sexuality? Promiscuous, perhaps? That's what you'd have us believe, isn't it? That you're wearing all that slap because you're meeting your boyfriend after school, or a group of admirers all waiting to ask you out,' James paused to breathe, then leaned in towards Laura and hissed, 'when really, you're nothing but a stupid little girl who's been playing with her mother's make-up.' James finished, red-faced, and stood back, proud. It was only then that he noticed she was crying.

'I'll get you back for this. Just you wait,' she spat, before running out of the room to hide her tears.

James stood shocked, his self-satisfaction quickly evaporating. The class was silent – some were appalled, some impressed. He paused, his eyes darting frantically from pupil to pupil, then he shot out of the classroom after her.

He knew she'd be in the Year 11 toilet, which, for reasons James had never understood, was a sanctuary to the girls. He hesitated outside, then looked around guiltily before pushing open the door.

'Laura?' he ventured, almost hoping she wouldn't be there, as he glanced about him for people that might jump to conclusions as to why he was standing in the doorway of the girls' bathroom. He heard muffled sobbing and a 'Go away!' from one of the cubicles. He closed the door behind him and loitered uncomfortably beside the Tampax dispenser. 'Laura, I'm sorry. I didn't mean what I said,' he muttered.

'Why did you say it, then?' she snapped from behind a locked door.

'I didn't mean to. It was just, well, all the things you said . . . You can't imagine how hard it is to gain the respect of a class when you're being bullied by a fifteen-year-old girl . . .'

'If you allow yourself to be bullied by a fifteen-year-old girl, you don't deserve respect.'

'Laura, I became a teacher because I wanted to make a difference in young people's lives. I'm not the bad guy.'

'Bullshit.' The sobbing had subsided and been replaced by intermittent snivels. After a moment of silence, James heard the bolt being slid back and the door opened. Laura emerged, her face red and blotchy, her nose and eyes swollen, streams of black mascara trickling lazily down her cheeks.

'Another disadvantage of make-up, huh?' She smiled between sniffs. James winced guiltily and instinctively wiped away a smudge of mascara with his thumb.

His hand lingered on her face far longer than it needed to, sparks jumping, crackling, between their skins. Her eyes grew wide, still glazed with tears, but he dared not meet her gaze. He traced the salty trails down her cheek with his index finger and brushed away the tears with the back of his hand.

He broke the silence. 'See? You don't need make-up.' The pair of them involuntarily jumped apart. Then quieter, 'You're beautiful without it.'

She was. He'd just never looked at her that way before. Her eyes were amazing – blue, green, hazel, grey, flecked with yellow. Her hair shone, but was tousled where she pushed it off her face. He yearned to reach out and smooth it. He winced at the wrong-ness of his thoughts and drew back, awkward, staring at the tiled floor. Her shoes were non-uniform.

He sighed and looked up. She was closer than he remembered. He watched, numb, as she reached out and touched his cheek. She cupped his face and stood on tiptoes to kiss him, gently, softly. So softly that it could have just been her breath on his lips. Her eyes shone, honest, longing. There was a brief pause and they lunged simultaneously, their lips meeting almost magnetically. His hands were in her hair, around her waist, hers on his back and face. At one point, James thought he could not tell where his body ended and hers began.

Class 11B were still sitting at their desks an hour later when the bell went for the start of break. And Mr Welsh was still sitting in the loos an hour and fifteen minutes later when break ended and he could slip out unnoticed.

James didn't work on Wednesday. He liked to think it was in appreciation of French culture, but really it was because there were an unusually small number of history GCSE classes this year and his tutor group had no lessons that day. James and Laura had not met again the previous day, though he did linger a little longer than usual outside the school gates in the hope that she might pass. Wednesday was supposedly the day for planning his lessons for 11B on Thursday and Friday, but thinking about 11B made him think about Laura, and thinking about Laura made him think about the events of the previous day. Consequently, he got no work done at all.

At one o'clock he gave up. He swept his untouched papers to one side and sat down to a lunch of chocolate biscuits and toast. He couldn't eat. Hunched pathetically over his plate, James reflected that he hadn't behaved this way since he was seventeen, and convinced he was in love with a girl called Kirsty . . . yes, it was Kirsty. This thought appalled, but also excited, James. He was drawn back to the covert encounters and first furtive fumbling of adolescence. For him, the day before had been nostalgic, but for Laura it was just the beginning. Suddenly, James felt incredibly protective of Laura, almost paternal. He knew what teenage boys were like. He'd been one, after all, and he didn't trust them with Laura. His Laura.

James paused, shook his head as if to clear his thoughts, and, shocked by the force of his emotion, made himself a very strong cup of coffee.

He thought he'd dreamed about Laura. He woke up with her face imprinted on his mind, but that was all.

This morning, there was a reason to get out of bed. History with 11B. First period. Obviously, nothing would occur in the lesson itself, but just seeing her would be a relief.

James got to school well in time for the start of first period. With a vague sense of unease in his stomach, James stepped into the room. It was unnaturally quiet, the class seated, a tense humidity hanging in the air. He looked around: Laura wasn't there. A few of the girls stared at him accusingly. With a wave of perverse relief, he realised that they probably suspected she was absent today because of the incident in class on Tuesday. He had no idea where she was.

Ten minutes later, the door swung violently open and Laura stormed in, claiming that her bus had been delayed. James looked at her, astonished, and thought he saw her wink, subtly. He caught on.

'Detention this afternoon, Laura, and stay behind after class, please.' He bit his lip to keep a straight face, and Laura beamed at him behind her hair. The rest of the lesson was, for James, spent in the backward shadow of what was yet to come.

The next days, weeks, maybe even months, passed in a honey-glazed, rose-tinted daze. The staff were amazed by Mr Welsh's newfound ability to control Miss Collins and by the sudden improvement in her history grades, despite getting regular detentions.

It was a dark and rainy Thursday evening in early December when James emerged from school and saw Laura standing by the gates. She was soaked but effortlessly beautiful, her dark hair clinging limply to her face. She greeted him with a gentle, lingering kiss, then took his hand and led him to his car. 'I thought it was about time I saw where you live.' She smiled, an ulterior motive glittering in her eyes. Still, he did not protest. They climbed into the car and listened to the raindrops pound on the roof of his old Metro for a moment. She slid her hand on to his knee.

'Someone might see us,' he whispered, half hoping they would.

'No, it's too late for anyone else to be here, and I told my parents I was staying over at a friend's to work on a science project. It's the perfect crime!' She grinned. James smiled back, though not quite as sure.

They drove to the flat in silence, James's attention focused on her hand on his thigh, burning, even through his suit. He was amazed to get home without causing a road accident. The flat was, as always, in a bit of a state. If Laura was bothered, she didn't show it as she picked her way through. They stood in a patch of clear and embraced one another.

Laura sighed in quiet contentment as she rested her head on his shoulder, then shivered. James looked up. 'God, girl. You're drenched; you must be freezing.' He rubbed her arms to try and warm her up.

'Yeah, I think I might take a shower,' she suggested and proceeded to the bathroom, leaving the door slightly open as an invitation. James boiled the kettle with nervous excitement, noting that this was just how he had felt when anticipating losing his virginity.

Steam drawn with eucalyptus, rolled out of the bathroom, and, in this mist, Laura appeared. She wore only a towel, held loosely around her breasts. Her hair shone like black honey, hanging on her shoulders and collarbone, dripping into her cleavage. In one movement she dropped the towel and stood motionless before him, smiling. 'Teach me.'

As James tried to sleep that night, one image flickered through his mind and kept him awake. Laura's face as they began – frowning in pain, tears glazing her eyes, her top teeth holding her bottom lip. He had held her and shushed her and offered to stop, but he felt it wasn't enough; he couldn't hold her close enough, he couldn't make that pain go away. He thought back. It hadn't hurt Kirsty that much, had it?

He rolled over and put his arms around her, stroking her breasts and stomach, his head buried in her shoulder. 'I love you.'

'I love you too.'

She reached up and stroked his hair. Their bodies merged, sealed by sweat and contentment. They slept.

James woke the next morning in an empty bed. He got up and wandered through to the kitchen. Laura was making toast and tea, wearing one of his shirts over her underwear. It was all scarily domestic.

Smuggling Laura into school was surprisingly easy. He let her out of the car a block from school and she walked the rest of the way, pretending to meet him by the gates so they could walk in together.

But Laura started when she opened the main door: her mother was standing by the office, gesturing wildly at the deputy head. James squeezed her hand behind her back and headed off before anyone saw him.

All through registration he fretted. Laura's mother must have rung her friend and found she wasn't there. What would she say? What would happen to them, to him? He was unsurprised when an office worker accompanied him to the head's office a half hour later. As he was led in, he passed Laura and her mother. Mrs Collins scowled furiously, Laura looked up briefly as he passed, crying hysterically. James paused and something made him look back – her eyes flickered momentarily, like a lizard's, and he saw something in her face that took him back to that Tuesday, some time ago now. 'I'll get you back for this. Just you wait' echoed in his head, uninvited.

Now, faced with charges of rape and sexual assault on a minor, as well as losing his job and the end of his teaching career, he couldn't help but wonder . . . She had been right – it was the perfect crime.

The Reunion

Sara Freeman

The Reunion

Hannah Richardson waved to her parents as they drove down the driveway. She sighed. It had taken her ages to convince them that she would be fine at home on her own.

They were only going to be away for a week, but they wanted to take Hannah with them. Hannah had refused. A boring business meeting, all week, with her stuck bored at some hotel. She didn't think so! She was old enough to look after herself; she was seventeen, after all.

She sat down on the sofa and glanced at the grandmother clock 11.30 a.m. Tim would be here soon. Tim was her boyfriend – light brown hair and dark blue eyes – Hannah considered him perfect.

She ran upstairs and changed into jeans and sweatshirt and tied her long brown hair into a ponytail. She wandered outside and got into her Porsche Boxster. She drove along the winding roads and soon came to the centre of Greenville village.

She got out of the car. She walked into the corner shop and bought some food to cook dinner for Tim and her.

As she was paying she had the feeling of being watched. She'd had these feelings for weeks, but she hadn't mentioned anything to her parents because they would never have let her stay on her own. Ignoring the feeling, she walked out of the shop and went back to her car.

On her way home, Hannah turned the radio on so that she could sing along. Glancing in her wing mirror, Hannah noticed a car behind her. Strange, considering there was only Hannah's house up this road.

She slowed down so that the car would overtake her. It didn't. She started to feel worried, then she saw her house. Relaxing a bit, she put her foot down and swerved into the driveway. She jumped out of her car and waited for the vehicle that had been behind her to go past. It never did.

Convinced she must have missed the car going past, Hannah made her way into the house. She began to prepare the meal she was planning to have with Tim. There was a knock at the door. Tim was early.

Hannah ran to the door and pulled it open. She smiled and asked Tim in. As they sat eating dinner, Tim looked across the table and commented, 'You're quiet.'

'Oh, it's nothing,' Hannah reassured him, not wanting to tell him about the car incident in case he thought that she was being paranoid.

That afternoon, they went ice-skating. Afterwards,

when Tim dropped Hannah back at home, the first thing Hannah did when she got inside was check the answer machine, her parents had probably phoned.

The first message was from her parents. 'Hi Hannah, we arrived safely. Wish you were here! Don't eat too much junk food. Give us a ring tomorrow. Bye!' Her mum's chirpy voice rang out from the machine and Hannah smiled and turned to go out of the room.

But there was a second message.

'I'm watching you, Hannah.'

Hannah whirled around and stared hard at the answering machine. She stormed over to it and played the message again.

Feeling frightened, she deleted it. Who had that been? Someone trying to be funny? Well, it wasn't. Especially after the way she had been feeling! The phone rang and she jumped. She picked it up, trying to keep her hand from shaking.

'Hello?' she answered cautiously.

Silence.

'Hello, is anyone there?' Hannah felt cross now.

'I'm watching you, Hannah. I know you're alone. Go look in your bedroom, there's a surprise waiting for you . . .' The raspy voice gave a chuckle.

Hannah slammed the phone down.

She climbed the stairs, but as soon as she saw her bedroom door she felt like running away. She tiptoed towards it, and paused before opening it. She grabbed a vase from beside her, threw open the door and flicked the light on.

She gave a sigh of relief as she walked in. There was nothing, nothing at all! She turned to go out, saw what was on the wall, and screamed.

The word 'DIE' was written all over the wall in chalk. Hannah raced down the stairs and into the lounge. Convinced that it wasn't a prank now, she picked up the phone and dialled Tim's number.

'Hello?' answered Tim.

'Tim, you've got to come, it's awful, oh Tim . . .' Hannah burst into tears.

'What's the matter? Are you OK?' Tim sounded worried.

'Oh, Tim, please come quick . . .'

'OK, I'm coming, stay right where you are . . .' He hung up.

Hannah put the receiver down, and didn't stop crying until Tim arrived. She opened the door and practically threw herself into his arms, so relieved that he was there to protect her. She showed him to the bedroom, but didn't go in with him. She simply stood outside the door, waiting for his reaction.

'Hannah!' Tim exclaimed in disbelief, 'Do you have any idea who would have done such a thing?'

'No, and that's what's frightening me,' Hannah told him. She then mentioned the phone calls.

'Well, we'll wipe this mess off,' Tim told her. 'It looks like someone was just playing a sick joke. But if anything else happens, phone the police or me. Shall I stay over tonight?'

'I'll be fine,' Hannah reassured him, but her voice shook slightly.

Tim gave her a concerned look, but didn't say anything as he left.

* * *

The intruder that was crouched in Hannah's garden smiled as Tim left, and turned to watch Hannah wave goodbye from the porch. The intruder left the grounds smirking, for after all, this was only the beginning.

* * *

Feeling better in the morning, Hannah had a relaxing shower, and then breakfast. Not wanting to be on her own she decided to go swimming, and then to McDonalds. She spent the afternoon shopping for clothes, and it was 6.00 p.m. when she decided to set off for home.

As she drove, she checked her rear-view mirror constantly. She laughed nervously, telling herself not to be so silly, and turned up the radio to calm her nerves. When she got home she turned on as many lights as possible in the house, and phoned Tim and spoke to him for half an hour. Then she phoned her parents, but she didn't tell them what had happened. She didn't want them worrying, and she wanted to prove to them that she was fine on her own.

Suddenly Hannah remembered her mobile. She ought to check it. She wandered into her bedroom looking for her mobile on the dressing table where she'd left it. It wasn't there. She was sure it had been there last night. She searched everywhere, but couldn't find it.

The phone rang downstairs, and she went to answer it.

'Hello?' she answered.

Silence

'Hello? Is anyone there?' she asked.

'Take a look outside . . .' the whispering voice said, laughing, and then the line went dead.

Hannah froze and dropped the receiver. But then anger surged up in her. Who was doing this? Annoyed and determined to stop this sick joke right now, Hannah raced to the front door and threw it open. She was gambling on her attacker expecting her to get scared. Well, she wasn't.

As the door flung open, Hannah prepared to confront the attacker. She took a deep breath, but it was knocked out of her when she saw what was outside the door. There was no one, just a large box. Puzzled, she bent to see what it contained.

She gasped.

Inside was a bunch of flowers. Dead flowers. But the card was even more disturbing. It read, *'You're next'*.

Hannah screamed and ran into the house. She grabbed the fallen receiver to dial the police. The line was dead.

'What?' Hannah whacked the phone on the table, and put her ear to it, no dialling tone.

She panicked and threw the phone down. Calm down and think, she told herself. This isn't going to get you anywhere! OK, she thought, there's a weirdo after me, wanting me dead, I can't phone anyone . . . but I still have transport! Hannah grabbed her keys. She had to get out of there, she decided.

She ran outside, leaving the front door open, and avoiding the dead flowers. She tripped and fell, bruising her knee. She pulled herself back up, swearing, and ran for her car.

Remembering the phone incident, she prayed silently to herself that the car would start as she put the keys in the ignition. It did. She gave a sigh of relief and backed out of the driveway. She sped down the road, ignoring the speed limit, scattering leaves and stones as she went. She glanced at her watch, 8.30 p.m. It would take her five minutes to get to Tim's house.

When she looked at her petrol gauge, she gasped. It was nearly empty! But that was impossible! She had filled it up earlier. Someone had taken the petrol out, she realised, and, as if confirming her suspicion, the car engine gave out a moan and the car slowed to a stop.

Hannah hit the car dashboard in frustration. What was she to do now? Walk, she decided; she couldn't just stay there. After about a minute of walking she thought she heard a rustling behind her, she whirled around and felt something whack her head. She felt an explosion of pain, and, unable to hold herself up, she felt herself falling.

Everything went black.

* * *

Hannah awoke feeling immense pain in her wrists, ankles, and head. She waited for her eyes to focus. She was in her living room! Someone had tied her up. She tried to move her hands. It was useless.

She was sitting on a chair, in the middle of the room. She wasn't gagged, but Hannah knew that was unnecessary. Who would hear her screaming? No one lived anywhere near her house.

There was no sign of her attacker. Why were they doing this? And how did they expect to get away with it?

Hannah must have lost consciousness again, because when she awoke and opened her eyes this time, she saw two eyes looking back at her. The rest of the person's face was covered. Something about the eyes spooked her. Had she seen them before?

This time she did scream, but she stopped when she heard laughing. It was dark in the room and Hannah had lost sight of the eyes. The attacker could be anywhere, she realised, feeling terrified.

'What's so funny?' she demanded.

Silence.

Hannah panicked. Where was the attacker?

'This isn't funny. What do you want?' Hannah's voice cried into the darkness.

The person started chuckling.

'Please, who are you?' Hannah whispered.

No answer.

'Show yourself!' screamed Hannah.

'You really don't know who I am?' The voice couldn't hide surprise. 'Well, perhaps I can give you a reminder . . .'

The lights flashed on and Hannah braced herself. But seeing the person in front of her still gave her a shock.

'Who the hell *are* you?' cried Hannah, shutting her eyes to block out the face she had seen.

She now realised why the eyes had spooked her – what they reminded her of and why she felt she had seen them before. She saw them in the mirror every-day. Her attacker was the mirror image of herself. Hannah forced herself to open her eyes. She had calmed down a bit and noticed some differences between her and the girl. Her attacker's hair was shorter, but they were so alike it was scary.

'Recognise me now?' the girl asked.

Hannah shook her head, tears spilling out.

'Haven't your parents ever mentioned me?' The girl's voice began to shake.

Hannah shook her head again. 'Why do you look like me?' she whispered. 'Who are you?'

'I'm your twin . . .' the girl answered angrily.

'But I don't have a twin . . .' Hannah told her.

'You don't know a thing about me?'

Hannah shook her head.

The girl sat opposite Hannah and took a deep breath. Hannah avoided her eyes, mainly because she was trying to loosen the rope around her hands and because she couldn't bear to look at them. This girl was a psychopath, she decided, and she had to get away.

'Before we were born,' the girl started, 'our parents had money problems. They couldn't afford to have two children and they knew a couple who were desperate for a child, so they agreed to let the couple have one of us. We were born and I was the one they gave away. *Me*. I was named Helen. You were born first so our parents decided to keep *you*.

'I lived with my adoptive parents for sixteen years before I found out the truth. I found my birth certificate. They told me everything and I found out I had a sister, so I tracked you down. It took a long time but I found you. Your life was so much better than mine. I loved my adoptive parents, but our biological parents had become successful and *you* had the life that I wanted. The life I could have had. So I devised a plan.'

Hannah kept working on the rope. She could see that Helen was losing control.

Helen started to stroke Hannah's hair, but Hannah pulled out of her grasp.

Plan, Hannah thought, what does she mean, *plan*? Hannah had almost got her hands free. She spotted a knife and fork on the table from her dinner the night before and she planned to use it if things got nasty.

'It must have been terrible for you,' Hannah empathised.

'TERRIBLE?' screamed Helen, 'What would *you* know? How could you possibly understand?'

'I'm sorry, but it isn't my fault,' Hannah whispered.

'Oh, but it *is*! If you hadn't been born first, none of this would have happened!' Helen yelled. 'But that's all going to change now . . .'

'What do you mean?' asked Hannah, her voice shaking.

'Once we have switched places, that is.' Helen smiled at her.

'Switched places?'

'Yes,' Helen repeated, 'I'll be Hannah and you can be Helen. Our parents would never know the difference. Not even the hair – I'll just say I cut it over the weekend. Do you like the idea?'

'No!' screamed Hannah, panicking. She had to get out of there! Luckily the rope had become loose enough for her to get her hands out.

'I didn't think you would like my idea,' Helen said, shrugging, 'which is why I'm going to have to get rid of you . . .'

'Let me go, and I'll forget this ever happened. Go home, think about the situation. Please, just let me go.'

'I can't do that,' she told her. 'Not when I've got this far. Not now.'

Helen got up and turned around.

Hannah grabbed the opportunity and got up slowly, trying not to catch Helen's attention. She reached for the knife on the table.

She grabbed it and leaned down to cut the ropes around her ankles. It was hard work, but she managed it. Luckily Helen was still facing the other way, muttering crazily to herself. Hannah sat back down and pretended she was still tied up, and it was just in time, as Helen whirled around.

Hannah stared at her hard. Helen really had flipped. Hannah wondered what her life would have been like if her parents had given her away instead. Would she have felt like Helen? She couldn't help feeling sorry for her.

Suddenly she realised that Helen wasn't looking at her, but was focusing on the table. Would she notice that the knife had gone?

'Wasn't there a knife on that table . . . ?' Helen inquired, looking at Hannah intently.

Hannah leapt at Helen. She didn't want to use the knife, but she might not have a choice.

'NO!' cried Helen, trying to dodge out of the way, but Hannah caught her and they fell to the ground. Hannah gripped the knife. She really didn't want to go through with it, but she was sure that if Helen had the knife she wouldn't be thinking twice about it.

They both scrambled off the ground and faced each other.

'Don't do this!' Helen cried. 'All I want is my parents . . .' Tears ran down her face.

'What do you expect me to do? You wanted to kill me!' cried Hannah.

'I'll go away . . . I won't come back.' Helen begged and got down on to her knees.

'You disgust me,' Hannah said, although she was glad she didn't have to use the knife.

She ran towards the door. Just as she reached it,

she heard a scream, and turned in time to see Helen lunge at her.

As they tussled, the knife fell and spun away across the floor.

'Get off me!' screamed Hannah, struggling to get up.

'I'm claiming what should have been mine!' Helen screamed back, trying to reach the knife.

At last they were free of each other and both raced for the fallen knife.

Epilogue

Mrs Richardson called for her daughter to hurry up. It was Hannah's eighteenth birthday, and seeing as she and Mr Richardson had been away a lot lately, they had decided to throw her a proper party. No doubt, Mrs Richardson thought, Hannah was checking her hair.

Hannah appeared at the top of the stairs. She looked wonderful in her new sparkling silver dress. Hannah smiled at her mum.

Her mum returned the smile, but she felt goose-bumps prickle her skin, even though it wasn't cold. She'd felt like this before; in fact, she'd felt this way ever since she and her husband had returned last month from a business trip. There was something different about Hannah, but she couldn't put a finger on it.

Family Business

Stephen Humphrey

Family Business

Jerome Jackson drew back the threadbare curtains of his South London flat and looked out on to the dawning Tuesday morning. The sun was just peeking nervously over the horizon. If the sun had a conscience, Jerome thought, then it would never rise; the rising of the sun brings the new day, and each new day brings death and suffering to many.

Jerome smiled to himself. He didn't often get philosophical, but he liked it when he did. Reluctantly shaking himself free of his melancholy reflections, he again assessed the promised day. There were no clouds in the sky at present. It looked like it would be a nice day. Strange to think, Jerome thought, that on so beautiful a day, a man was going to die. And that he was going to kill him.

He'd risen early to give himself time to prepare, physically and mentally. Going across to the single ragged armchair in his sparse, unkempt flat, Jerome sat down and reflected on the previous night's meeting with Don Cezano.

* * *

Jerome Jackson was a hitman for the Cezano Family,

one of the four powerful Mafia families in the United Kingdom. The head of the Family, the Don, had brought his fledgling family to the UK from his native Sicily many years ago, when he himself was a mere twenty-one years old. Masquerading as a legitimate and respectable jeweller, Don Cezano had built up a strong and powerful Family, surrounded by his four sons, each in charge of a number of men ready to do the Don's bidding. Jerome was under the regime of Pete Cezano. The man closest to the Don, his *consigliori*, was Gioberti Noto. He was the Don's closest friend, counsellor, advisor, and had a law degree which occasionally came in useful. Jerome had never met Noto, but he was almost as legendary as the great Don himself. Almost.

The Cezano Family had tight controls on gambling throughout the country. It was their speciality, their particular area of interest. The other three UK Families dealt with drugs, smuggling, and other affairs that held no interest for the Don. Whilst based in Birmingham, the Don's power extended to London, Manchester, Glasgow, and certain smaller operations in the South West.

On Monday afternoon, Pete Cezano had arrived at Jerome's flat.

Jerome liked Pete. Pete was thirty-one, just four years older than Jerome. He was short, taking after his mother rather than his father in that respect. He had thick, jet-black hair, and a bad habit of wearing Hawaiian shirts and large, garish pieces of jewellery.

'The Don wants to see you urgently, Jerome,' Pete said.

'Just me?'

'Just you. At seven o'clock this evening.'

'I can't get to Birmingham in that time,' Jerome protested.

Pete smiled. 'He's already in London. He'll meet you in the jeweller's shop in Oxford Street at seven o'clock. Don't be late, Jerome.'

After this short interview, Pete had left. Jerome poured the remaining beer in the can he'd been drinking down the sink. He would need a clear head to meet the Don.

As he got ready, he didn't once try to imagine what the Don wanted to see him about. He'd been with the Family for some years now, and knew that the Don would tell you everything he wanted you to know when he wanted you to know it.

Jerome arrived outside the jeweller's shop three minutes before seven. This was the legitimate face of the Family. The glittering, sparkling wares in the window were hidden from view by the metal grille pulled down to protect them. The grille that blocked the door to the shop was also down, but not quite all the way. Seconds later, a hand from within the shop appeared beneath the grille and pushed it up. It was Pete.

'Punctual. That's good.' He smiled, standing back to allow Jerome in. Then he pulled down the metal grille and closed the door behind them.

As he walked through the shop, Jerome looked around him at the vast array of diamonds and rings and necklaces. Within a glass cabinet in the centre of the shop floor was a diamond and ruby-encrusted tiara. One cabinet was full of watches that each probably cost more than a whole year's rent for Jerome's flat. They stopped outside the door leading to the back office. Pete looked at his watch.

'Ten seconds,' he said. 'Smarten yourself up.'

Jerome cleared his throat, smoothed down his hair, and made sure his shirt was tucked in.

'Seven o'clock,' Pete said. 'You're on.'

Jerome turned the door handle, and entered the office.

The manager of this shop clearly didn't keep many personal effects in his office. No pictures on the walls, or any personal touches anywhere. Just several filing cabinets, a computer, a couple of leather chairs, and a desk. Behind this desk sat the Don. In a chair in a corner of the office sat Noto.

'Mr Jackson,' said the Don, in his very British, almost affected, accent. 'Please, take a seat.'

Jerome did as he was asked, taking one of the chairs opposite the Don.

'Drink?' the Don asked. 'I believe my manager keeps

a bottle of fine whisky in one of these drawers . . .'

'No, thank you,' Jerome replied.

The Don seemed satisfied with this answer. Slightly to his right was an unopened bottle of still mineral water. The Don did not smoke, or drink alcohol. He ate sparingly, but well. Every day, he strolled around the Cezano Family compound in Birmingham, a good five-mile walk in all. He was sixty-five years old, but looked just a little over fifty. His distinguished, white-silver hair was cut short, and he wore a grey pinstripe suit. His eyes were a warm, inviting brown. His teeth were all his own, and a dazzling white. The only hint of age was the slender black cane resting before him on the desk, which he sometimes used if the arthritis in his left hip was acting up. This seldom happened, but he always carried the cane. Jerome suspected he used it to fool people into believing that he really was an old, weak man. Nothing could be further from the truth. Legend had it that only a year ago, the Don had broken a man's neck with his bare hands. Looking into the clean-shaven, smiling face now, it was hard to believe that such a genial-looking man could do anything of the kind, but Jerome knew how vital deception was within the Families.

'You've been with the Family for five years now,' the Don said, a statement of fact more than a question.

'Yes, sir.'

'Under the regime of my son Pete,' Don Cezano went on. 'He tells me you are reliable, efficient, and loyal. Excellent attributes in a trusted employee. I could use more men like you in my other sons' regimes.'

Don Cezano's face broke into a wide smile. Jerome remained silent.

'You are the best I have right now, Jerome,' the Don said, seriously, the smile quickly fading. 'And I need the very best for what I have planned.'

Opening the bottle of water and taking a sip, the Don pushed a photograph across the desk to Jerome.

'Do you recognize that man?' he asked.

'Julian Soames,' Jerome said, examining the photo. 'Eminent politician, a member of the Cabinet. Doing a little business with us, wasn't he?'

'He was,' the Don replied. 'However, our Mr Soames is proving to be more dangerous and foolish than I had anticipated. We helped him out when his gambling debts became too big to handle. He couldn't pay them off, and was concerned that if he didn't, the story would get leaked to the press. He came to us, and I cancelled his debts wherever I had influence. You know how the Mafia works, of course?

'You do a favour for someone free of charge, and they offer you their friendship in return, and will one day do you a service when required,' Jerome said. He knew how the Mafia worked.

'Precisely. A man in the Cabinet would have proved most useful. However, Soames doesn't appear to understand how the arrangement works. Three days ago, he came to me with a proposition. Some Colombian friends and he were smuggling a large consignment of drugs into the country. He wanted me to put up half the capital, that is, one million pounds, and also use my influence in the London Dockland Authority to get them to turn a blind eye.

'I refused. I am a family man, Mr Jackson, and I know the damage drugs can do. My business is gambling. Always has been, and always will be. Drugs are a messy business, of which I will have no part. I told Soames this, and he left.'

'Wait a second,' Jerome said. 'Did I read something in the papers yesterday about a consignment of drugs being seized by the Dockland Authority?'

The Don nodded. 'Quite likely you did. It was Soames's little plan that went awry. He was clever enough to distance himself from the operation, so he's not been exposed yet. He was foolish enough, however, to accuse me of tipping off the LDA. That is something I would never do. I disagreed with his plan, but I am a man of honour, and would not betray a confidence. They were caught because their operation was badly thought through, and doomed to fail from the very start. Nevertheless, Soames came to me and threatened to expose the Family. That is something I cannot allow.'

Jerome could now see where this was going.

'So far, Soames has kept quiet,' Don Cezano went on. 'He's an MP. He doesn't want to draw any attention to himself. But we have no way of telling how long he will keep silent for. It's too risky, Jerome. I want you to kill Soames.'

Jerome remained silent. The Don had more to say.

'Ever since we did business with Soames the first time, we've been watching him with some interest. We have found out that our distinguished MP is having an affair with a girl in Kensington. Three times a week, he goes to her flat and spends the morning there. Tomorrow is one of those days. To pay back our politician, and expose his torrid little affair, I want you to shoot him on the steps of the flat.

'As we speak, my son Thomas is parking a van across the road from the flat. It is a stolen white van with falsified licence plates. The manufacturer's label has been removed, so there are no reliable means of identifying or tracing the van. The keys will be waiting for you at your flat when you get home. Once you shoot Mr Soames, you will get into the van and drive off as fast as possible. Go to Southampton. There, you can leave the van. No one will be able to trace it. Then, you'll catch a ferry to Sicily. I have men there waiting for you. You will stay there until it is safe to return.

The Don stopped. There was a silence as Jerome let it sink in.

'A very high-profile killing,' he said, after a while.

'Mmm.' The Don nodded, as he sipped his water. He replaced the plastic bottle on the desk. 'The murder of a Cabinet Minister is going to get a lot of attention. That is why we need you out of the country as soon as possible. I have friends and associates in Sicily who will see you are well looked after until you can return. Pete will give you the details this evening, after you leave.'

The Don stood up, and Jerome did the same. They shook hands.

'Thank you, Jerome Jackson,' the Don said, smiling. 'What you are doing for the Family will not be forgotten.'

'I would do anything for the Family,' Jerome assured him.

As he turned to leave the office, the Don said something that was to stick in Jerome's mind for a long time.

'It must be a perfect crime,' he said. 'There must be no way of linking it to the Family. Remember that. A *perfect* crime.'

The rest of the evening was spent with Pete in Jerome's flat, going over the details – what weapon to use, what ferry to catch and when, how the Family would contact him in Sicily and update him with developments in England, and so on. At ten-thirty, Pete had left and Jerome had gone to bed. He slept soundly. His work never kept him awake at night.

* * *

And now here he was, he thought. Sitting in an old armchair, staring at the garish red numbers on the digital clock. He would have to start getting ready.

After washing, Jerome got dressed in front of the mirror. Pete had instructed him to wear the least conspicuous clothes possible, so as not to draw attention to himself. But Jerome had known to do that anyway. Pete was just jittery because this hit was so important.

The gun he was to use was loud. Any onlookers must realise exactly what was going on, and the noise would scare them away from Jerome and prevent any attempts at heroic intervention on the public's part. It would fit comfortably in his jacket pocket.

After he pulled his rust-red pullover down over his head, he looked at his reflection in the mirror. Long brown hair, a moderately thick brown beard, and a crooked nose where it had been broken in a fight some years before. In that same fight, he'd lost one of his front teeth. It had been replaced with a false tooth. He also needed glasses, but usually wore contact lenses instead. For the shooting, he would wear glasses, and remove his false tooth. Long hair, a beard, glasses, and a tooth missing – these were the details witnesses would pick up on. And they could all be altered. When in Sicily, he would replace the false tooth, shave off his beard, have his hair cut short and bleached blond, and return to wearing contacts. Maybe he'd even get surgery done to straighten his nose? With or without that final, fine detail, he'd still be a completely different person to the one who shot Julian Soames, MP.

Content with his appearance, Jerome took a last, unemotional look at the miserable little flat, and then left to begin the long walk to Kensington.

There was a greengrocer's shop just opposite the girl-friend's flat. Jerome waited in the shop, looking out the window to watch for Soames. If Soames was true to routine, he would be leaving any minute now.

As Jerome was trying to look interested in a crate of kiwi fruit, he caught sight of the door to the flat opening. Swiftly, he left the shop.

Soames was saying goodbye to his girlfriend as he made his way down the steps. He was hidden beneath a long, dark raincoat and wore a trilby, pulled down to cover his face. But Jerome knew

Soames's picture well enough to recognise him. As Soames waved to his girlfriend, who was still standing in the doorway in her dressing gown, Jerome ran across the road to the foot of the steps. Taking the gun from his pocket, he aimed at Soames. The first bullet caught Soames's shoulder, knocking him to his knees. Its loud report sounded throughout the street, and Jerome heard the screams of onlookers. The second bullet got Soames in the throat, the third and forth lodged in his chest. The fifth hit the MP right in his forehead. Jerome fired the sixth and final shot into the air, to ward off bystanders.

Dropping the gun as he'd been instructed by Pete, Jerome swiftly ran to the white van parked on the corner. The people in the street were standing still and silent. The screams of Soames's girlfriend were the only thing piercing that silence.

Don Cezano, Pete and Noto were sitting in a café, at a window from which they could see the white van. The Don was the very epitome of cool, reading a newspaper, his bottle of still mineral water to his left, almost empty. Pete was far less composed, glancing out of the window every few seconds, drinking his strong black coffee in large swigs.

Hearing the shots, Noto smiled broadly.

'That's the end of our political problem,' he said quietly.

The Don gave a thin, weak smile before returning to his newspaper.

Pete watched as Jerome leaped into the driving seat of the van. A second later, as he turned the key in the ignition, the van exploded in a loud burst of red and orange flame. Pete closed his eyes, and bowed his head. He felt sick.

Don Cezano folded his newspaper and finished his bottle of water. Motioning to Pete, he got up to leave the café, Noto following close behind him.

'I still don't think we had to kill Jerome,' Pete hissed angrily, running to catch up with his father and the *consigliori* as they walked away from the café. He turned to look at the twisted, blackened, smouldering remains of the white van. 'He was a good and loyal man.'

'Even the strongest loyalty has its limitations,' Noto reminded him.

'Precisely. The only man who will not betray you, my son,' said the Don, wearily, 'is a dead man.'

The Perfect . . . Murder?

Maxine Kocura

The Perfect . . . Murder?

I never could stand that jerk Lucius. Stuck up and arrogant, he was. Still, I fixed him good in his turn. I remember thinking, when they were counting down the line, That's yours, Lucius. That's yours.

But I'm getting ahead of myself. It all started back in Britain. We were about to face a battle. I had spent the previous night sleeping on the cold, hard, damp British soil, trying to ignore the feeling of water seeping into my woollen blanket from the earth. We had camped on the edge of a forest. We never had forests like *that* one back in Rome. The trees were very dark and close together and, every so often, strange sounds floated through the mist towards our camp. The branches of the trees were gnarled, like the clawed hands of an old woman, and I could just imagine the trees' limbs coming to life and stretching out to tear my blanket away from me and scratch at my skin.

I know what you're thinking: Not a very brave way to behave for a Roman soldier. But I *was* scared. I was stuck in a hostile, unfamiliar country, longing for the warmth of the Roman sun on my back. How I missed it. As well as the fleeting longing for the past was the prolonged agony of dwelling upon the future.

At some point in the next day we would come across the first of the British resistance fighters. Before, opposition was thin, but we were no longer on the shores of an island. We were coming further and further into the centre, which the enemy dominated. They outnumbered us. Can you imagine? The pitiful, disorganised, pale British actually had a chance of winning. And now a quite different image was forming in each soldier's mind: the image of savage, ruthless warriors charging towards us. Images of me, being cut down by the enemy swords and stabbed to death by their spears.

We would die. Of that, we were certain. We were just soldiers. Infantry. The ordinary, expendable people who actually did the fighting while the emperors sat back and watched. What did it matter if the troops got cut down? They can just send in more. Who cared about each individual person? About their ambitions, about their hopes and, most importantly, about their fears.

That's what worried me most, as I lay there, tossing and turning and trying to find my way into the dark oblivion of sleep. Except I knew that when I slipped away I would be tormented further by the sinister shades of my nightmares. I knew that if I let my eyes shut, instead of imagining all those fierce, snarling faces and cold, cruel eyes, I would see them right in front of me. So I preferred to lie awake, agonising, pondering life and death, to watch the occasionally shaking back of the sentry as he sat staring out into the hazy fog of the gloomy forest.

After some time, I realised that I recognised him, even though all I could see of his wiry frame was the back of his head and his thin shoulders. His name was Quintus and he was the youngest. By all rights, he should still have been back at home, playing sports with his friends. He was a slight lad, no more than sixteen years of age, and I could tell that he was scared. In fact, if I leaned over to my right a little, I could see that the poor boy was in tears. The only thing that kept him from sobbing aloud was the fist he had wedged in his mouth to keep himself from waking the troops. Poor lad, I thought, he has prob- ably never even seen the sight of blood before. It occurred to me that, even though I was little more than eight years his elder, this was my first major battle too. Then it also occurred to me that I was his senior after all and probably wouldn't sleep at all anyway.

So I got up quietly, ignoring the sharp pain in my back from where a twig had jabbed me, and carefully picked my way through the sleeping camp. As I lifted my foot to step over a tightly wrapped bundle, it moaned in its sleep, perhaps having the same nightmares I had stayed awake to avoid. Strangely, I felt myself responsible for his torment, as if somehow, if I had fallen asleep, the same dark dreams would befall me instead of him. I carefully stepped over him. Another man, perhaps sensing movement nearby, rolled over and kicked the still hot embers of the fire with his bare foot. I winced. He grunted, but turned over. I had finally picked my way to the outskirts of the camp, where Quintus was still sitting, sobbing silently.

I moved up beside him, laid my hand on his shaking shoulder. He jumped, turned around, then scrubbed at his eyes with his grubby sleeve, ashamed.

'Hey there, son.' I greeted him softly. 'You doing all right?'

He sniffed, rubbed his eyes again, 'Yes sir. Fine sir.'

'Get some sleep,' I offered, 'I'll take it from here.'

The boy was grateful. He got up, and with another sniff, prepared to scuttle off. I stopped him with a hand on his arm.

'Son?'

'Yes sir?'

'You're gonna be fine.'

'Thanks, sir.'

He disappeared into the darkness.

Time passed. I don't know if it was minutes or hours, but the darkness did not give way to light, and the heavy mist that hung over our camp did not lift. Every so often the snores of the sleeping men drifted

towards me, and the fervent scuttle of a night creature shook me to my very bones. And soon I began
to feel a leaden weight, pulling my eyes shut.

The sound of a twig snapping jolted me from my
sleep-laden haze. I jumped, whirled clumsily around,
my battered sword half-drawn. A chuckle pierced
the silence.

'Relax, Marcus,' an annoyingly familiar voice
sneered, 'or soon you will be jumping at shadows.'

'Lucius.' The jerk.

He laughed again, at his own lame-but-hurtful
joke.

'What do you want?' I demanded. I hated him, so
arrogant and so sure of himself.

'What?' he asked with mock innocence. 'Since
when couldn't a wounded warrior have a little space
to sit and enjoy the warmth of the fire?'

The last comment was wry; the fire had long since
become just embers. He drew his sword and poked
through these embers to revive a small flame.

Lucius had been considered something of a hero
ever since the day before, when he had single-hand-
edly taken down a very small group of resistance
scouts sent to spy on us. He had acquired wounds to
the shoulder and leg, the latter being slightly more
serious.

'You replied to my question with a question,' I
said. 'What are you doing here?'

Again, that superior smile. 'My wounds have kept me up all night. Why bother tossing and turning when you can sit and keep watch.'

What? That last sentence was pointed; had he been watching *me*?

'Are you scared?' he asked outright.

'No!' I countered. Even to myself, my voice sounded painfully shrill. I recovered, slightly, and attempted to catch him out.

'Are *you* scared?'

'My dear Marcus,' he began, in a voice as sweet as honey (and deadly as an adder's bite), 'I have no need to be. Our honourable General has agreed to let me sit the battle out, as my leg wound would be too much of a bother.' He smiled slyly, examining his grimy nails as he carried on. 'Of course, this is also because he feels I have proved myself for the day. Have you done any heroic deeds recently? I think not. Therefore, I wish you good luck tomorrow.'

He fell silent. I did not reply. This was mainly because I couldn't think of a good comeback. Also because I felt that if he did not shut up, I would take my sword and stab him, right then. But slowly, through the silence, I could hear the soft voice of my conscience whispering, 'You're scared . . . you're scared.' It was about five minutes until I realised that it was not my conscience, but the quiet, sneering voice of Lucius whispering in my ear.

'I am not!' I cried, again sounding shrill. I knew that it just made me look even more cowardly, but I could not keep myself quiet. Apparently, he could, because the only reply he gave me was the same smug grin that I had grown so sick of in all the time I had known him. How I wanted to wipe it from his face. I would show him that I wasn't scared. I would . . .

Suddenly, a piercing shriek tore through the night air. I jumped, with a frightened gasp. They were coming for us, they would tear me limb from limb, and I was helpless against them . . . helpless.

Then I saw through my panicked haze that Lucius was laughing. I also saw the smudge of white against black as the owl flew overhead. I shuddered. Still recovering from my fright, I realised that Lucius was laughing at *me*. Oh, what an idiot I was. Jumping at birds was almost as bad as jumping at shadows, as he had suggested before. If only I could shut him up once and for all.

He stood up, wiped his tunic down.

'If mere fowl frighten you so, Marcus, then I would very much like to see you against the enemy tomorrow. Only if you stop jumping at shadows will you finally become a man.'

He melted into the night, which swallowed him up, but did not swallow the shame that I now felt deep in my breast.

* * *

The next morning, the camp rose early. It was strange to see it from this perspective – the camp, for once, waking to me, not I to the camp. One minute, everything was dark and silent, and the next it was light, and the camp was bustling to life. In truth, I was glad. I was happy to be free from the cold, black night, with its strange noises and ghostly apparitions. And shame. I could still remember Lucius's sneer from the night before. In fact, I could see it now as he strode up to me.

'Fine morning, eh, soldier?' he said cheerfully, though limping slightly on his bad leg. 'Not had much sleep?'

I then realised how awful I must have looked. My eyes were red from lack of sleep. My face was pale from worry and constant frights in the dark. My clothes were crumpled and stained and my hair was full of twigs. I was one shaky soldier.

'Go away!' I snapped. I probably could have thought of something better to say, had I not been in such a bad mood. To my annoyance, he shrugged calmly and strolled away. I scowled at his retreating back.

It was when I saw the grim faces of my comrades that I remembered why I had been so scared the night before. Today we would fight. We might win, but *I* might die.

* * *

We had been marching further and further into unknown land. The fog still hadn't lifted, so the General had sent out two scouts to go on ahead up a hill. My feet sunk into the thick mud, which splashed on my torn tunic, dulling yet another patch of off-white with brown. Oh, how I missed Rome. My breastplate hung heavily around my shoulders, weighing me down further and making my already heavy heart sink.

However, the worst was still to come. There was a noise up ahead. To my horror, the scouts came running back down the hill at top speed. They made straight for the General and started talking to him. Although I could not hear them, I could see their wild, scared eyes. I felt cold all over, and not because of the British climate. There was now another reason for the cold and sickness in the stomach that gripped us all: Over the top of the hill we could see the painted visages of the first British warriors charging at us. As they came closer, I could make out the individual details, just as if it were one of my nightmares. But this was all too real. I could now make out the woad patterns on their snarling faces. The General, calm as ever, gave the order to attack. But I just froze. We all did, transfixed by the horrifying scene of all those trained killers stampeding towards us. We all froze. Then we ran.

We ran like we had never run before. The fearless

Romans, come to conquer the pathetic Britons, running in their flimsy boots, feet slapping in the British mud, tortured lungs gasping the stale British air. We ran, and we did not even look back to see their smug, superior faces.

The trees were all around me, their crooked branches seemed to press in, tugging at my hair, just as I'd imagined they would. I had gone inside the forest to prove that I could.

'See, Lucius!' I cried aloud at the empty forest. A crow, startled from its perch, leapt into the sky, shrieking. 'I'm not afraid to go into the forest!'

I may have run, but so had everyone else. If Lucius had been there, he would have run too. Probably. Or maybe he would have charged out alone as he had with the enemy scout party, and killed them all. And he would have been made a general. This was all his fault. If he hadn't scared me the night before, broken me down, frightened me so much . . . I looked up into the forest. I could hardly see the sky. It was getting dark. I made my way back to camp.

When I returned, I saw the strangest sight. The whole troop, a hundred men, was lined up in a single row. The General was shouting at them. I stared for a moment, then one of the General's personal guards shoved me forward.

'Wait!' I cried. 'What's going on?'

The guard laughed mirthlessly. 'Get in line, soldier. Have you ever heard of decimation?'

My heart sank. Decimation. The typical Roman punishment for cowardice. Unfortunately, we seemed to have brought the tradition to Britain. If the army ran away from battle, they needed to be punished. But you couldn't kill a whole army, even though they were expendable. So instead, the general lined the army up and killed every tenth person as an example to the rest.

'Get in line!' the guard pushed me forward. I staggered on shaking legs. I scanned the line. Person number ten: Pilus . . . number twenty – my heart sank further: Quintus . . . number thirty: Otho . . . number forty – wait!

Person number twenty-nine: Lucius! The cause of my cowardice and suffering. I stormed over to him.

'Well, hello there,' he said dryly. 'It looks like even though I wasn't even *in* the "battle", I'm still part of the punishment. You'd think the honour I got yesterday would stop me from having to take part in the decimation . . . Seems not.'

I didn't reply. I was too angry. This was his fault. *All* his fault.

He smirked again, 'You scared?'

Oh, scared, am I? I could never stand you, Lucius. Stuck up and arrogant, you are.

A shout of agony from the beginning of the line, a guard standing over Pilus with a bloody spear.

'Well, are you scared?'

I'll fix you good.

Another scream, shriller this time. I turned just in time to see Quintus fix me with an accusing look before the blood bubbled out of his mouth and he died.

Like it was my fault. Like I had lied when I told him he'd be all right.

I looked down the line. Number twenty-nine: Lucius . . . number thirty: Otho . . .

'Are you scared, Marcus?'

Shut up. Shut up!

I began to sweat. Glistening droplets slid down my forehead and face like tears. I moved into place. Number twenty-nine: me . . . number thirty: Lucius . . . *That's yours, Lucius. That's yours!*

'Hey Marcus, don't worry. It's OK to be scared.'

That's yours. That's . . . What? Was he being kind or was he taunting me?

Lucius flashed me a reassuring smile, the brave man that he was. Then it changed into a look of pained surprise as the spear came down. He'd thought he was number twenty-nine.

But see, Lucius, the numbers changed when I came in. You hadn't bargained for that.

The guard moved down the row . . . I had Lucius's blood on me. I felt sick . . .

The last screams rang out, and then all was silent. The General spoke to us about something for a minute, but I didn't hear.

I had his blood on me. I had his blood on my *hands*.

I sank to my knees in the mud. I looked down through blurred eyes. Lucius's blood mingled with the soil, turning the ground red.

The guard came over to me. He was saying something. I didn't really hear it. 'Seen . . . much . . . probably in shock.'

'Up you get, son.'

The General. Everybody else had gone. He helped me to my feet and guided me to my sleeping space. But it just didn't seem real.

'He . . . didn't mean to be cruel . . . He was just being friendly. He was a good man . . . really . . . I'm . . . a . . . murderer.'

'Whatever you say, son,' the General said. He and the guard walked away. I sank down into my blanket.

And now, whenever I find my way into the dark oblivion of sleep, whenever I finally manage to slip away, I am still tormented by nightmares. But now, instead of the emotionless, angry, snarling faces of an enemy who are more animal than human, I see the pained surprise on the all-too-human face of a man, who, even though I caused his death, remained my friend until he breathed his last.

The Felines Versus RJ Bones

Máire MacNeill

The Felines Versus RJ Bones

Will I describe the events of that evening? Well, if you insist.

It was incredibly traumatising.

There I was, sitting in my fluffy grey basket, having just finished off a plate of fish, whilst my arch-enemy, Commanding Officer RJ Bones, out-and-out leader of the Hertfordshire Dogs Union, was outside in the pouring rain. He'd been banished for climbing over No Man's Land (the sofa) with muddy paws. The house was all mine. The Human had just gone out, and I was about to settle down for a nap. Oh yes, life was sweet.

The war between our two parties has been going on for as long as anyone can remember, certainly before either Bones's time or my own. Legend has it that it all came about when Great-Aunt Dixie scratched one of Bones's ancestors on the nose. A rumour among the ranks is that the canines have formed alliances with the mice. But who can say?

Anyway, back to that afternoon. I'd chalked (or should I say, scratched) another point on the wall for the FC (Feline Confederacy), and Bones had noticed. I could see him getting angrier by the moment. (The Human had recently had French windows fitted.) She's generally the peace-keeper between the two of us and rarely shows her bias, although she secretly prefers me; whilst *I* am free to come and go as I please, Bones is dragged around on a leash, and has even been taken to Gigi's Doggy Beauty Salon. (He's just a few steps away from becoming a poodle! Ha!)

Sorry, m'lud, I'll refrain from digressing.

I have to admit, it was partly my fault that he was locked outside. You see, we had agreed on a temporary truce whilst his strongest men were at the vet, but when he was about to jump up on to No Man's Land, I didn't mention that I could clearly see the Human coming through the Conference Room (a.k.a., the lounge, when we're not discussing issues of state). He jumped, she shouted, he got banished and I got Kitty-Kat. All's fair in love and war.

Anyway, Bones was understandably not amused. Well, who would be, really? After giving me the evil eye for about fifteen minutes, he finally realised that he was small enough to fit through my cat-flap, which wasn't locked. He's a smart one, that Bones. Who elected him Commanding Officer anyway?

I grew a little nervous when I heard him enter Battlefield A. It's understandable; I can usually hold my own in a fight with him, but I could see that he was out for blood – namely mine . . . sorry, I'll retract that . . . that he was extremely angry with the situation in which he had been placed, and was therefore more threatening towards me than usual. Although I say it myself, I showed remarkable bravery (and afterwards promoted myself to Field Marshall), and merely jumped up on to No Man's Land (not without a sense of dramatic irony) to defend myself.

'Bones,' I spat. Ordinarily, enemies at war address each other by their full titles, but as we are forced to share territory, a certain informality has evolved.

'Cat,' he spat back, just as nastily as I had, and I have to say that he was taking things a bit far. Most of the time, he does call me by my real name. I saw that he meant business, although at the time I *did* think that, if he really wanted a full-scale battle, he might have addressed me formally, at least for the sakes of our forefathers. (Pawfathers!)

I'm sorry, m'lud. It won't happen again, I promise.

As coolly as possible, I asked Bones what he wanted.

'I have a score to settle,' he told me, with an evil glint in his eye.

'With Skeletor,' I almost added, by way of a hilarious joke, but decided against it, and instead gave him a cynical look, to show that I was unable to believe that he was choosing to steal bad, clichéd lines from bad, clichéd, mid-eighties movies. (The Human likes to watch Channel 5.)

'And what do you intend to do?' I asked, cursing

my stupidity for breaking our staring contest (Rule 136 in the FC handbook: *A feline's stare is deadly. Humans and canines alike fear nothing more than being stared at unblinkingly*).

'Do we fight?' I went on.

'Something better,' he told me. 'I don't intend to take any of the blame from *her*,' meaning the Human, 'when she gets back. But I think you'll be . . . somewhat surprised when you see what I have in store for you.'

Then I noticed who had just entered the Conference Room.

'Meet my new back-up,' Bones said with an evil smirk.

It was Private Ginger, a young recruit to the FC. I was devastated. How could this have happened? I asked myself. I'd made Ginger the wing-child of one of my most reliable majors . . . this was inconceivable.

'Private Ginger's been working for me this whole time,' said Bones. 'He's a spy for our side. A very good one – for a cat – and very good at picking up all the details. Who'd have thought that one handbook could contain so much information?'

I felt ill. Ginger sneered at me. Traitor.

Although my pride had suffered a knock and the situation was sinking faster than the *Titanic*, I still asked, 'Well, what can Private Ginger do?'

Bones paused before he answered. He was loving every minute of this.

'Damage to the Conference Room that looks a lot more feline than I could ever do.'

After that, I can barely register what happened. Bones chased me into Battleground C, barking, keeping me cornered. Although I hissed and scratched for all I was worth, Bones was relentless, not letting me loose. In the meantime, Ginger got to work in the Conference Room.

When it was over, I sneaked back in. I was horrified by the sight of the Conference Room. There were papers everywhere, cushions on the floor and big scratch-marks all over the walls. Ginger had obviously rolled all over No Man's Land, as well as every other conceivable place, leaving dirt and bits of fur everywhere.

I was going to be skinned and made into violin strings when the Human got home.

When she did get home, I had hell to pay. Bones was curled up outside in his kennel, big brown eyes, wagging tail, clean fur (he'd dried himself off on the rug inside, taking care to leave a feline-sized wet patch) – the very image of canine goodness. I hid under a table, waiting guiltily. What else could I do?

My jingle-ball was confiscated immediately and I had no Kitty-Kat for a week (I had to make do with

Cat-U-Like). As well as that, I was sent outside, and, to add insult to injury, salt to the wound, fleas to the bad fur day, Bones was allowed back in.

I'm still in therapy.

It's a dog's life; no pun intended.

And that is all I have to say on the matter, m'lud.

A Deeper Shade of Love

Jenny Morgan

A Deeper Shade of Love

The rain beat down on the roof like a wild beast trying to get in. The radio was loud to drown the incessant drumming and the heater was coughing out torrents of tepid, musty air, but she was cold. Her parents had been arguing again, and as she sat next to her father in the front of the car, she could feel the anger radiating off him like steam from a kettle, and she was afraid. She caught a glimpse of her pregnant mother in the wing mirror, sitting huddled in the back, and she saw the tears streaming down her pale face. She turned back and, as the windscreen wipers licked away another sheet of water, she saw it. A great lake had formed on the side of the road and she barely had time to gasp before the steering wheel wrenched itself from her father's grasp and the car lurched like a bronco before veering off the lane. Tree branches whipped across the roof and she heard a window smash before she saw the wall looming in the dusky light. She had a vague sensation of complete silence and then the rending screech of metal filled her head. The car crumpled like a tin can and she was trapped. 'I don't want to die, I don't want to die,' she wailed, but the night closed its ears and turned its cold back.

I knew what happened next, for it happened every time my mind replayed the terrible night. I tried to prevent myself from doing it as I always did, but my will was barely stronger than my body. My eyes swivelled upwards from where I was cramped in the foot-hole, and I saw my dead mother's face looming over me. Her eyes were wild and terrified like a mad dog looking down the muzzle of a gun, and purple blood dripped on to the seat. I closed my eyes to block out the horror and wept.

The pain was bad this morning. He could see it coursing through her limbs and exploding inside her head. He watched as her little chest rose and fell heavily, willing her shallow and irregular breathing to even out. Her sallow face was moist with sweat and her eyes were dull under heavy lids. She was dreaming again, and any minute now she would awake with the same animal cries that had haunted him for two years now. She had been so full of life before the crash and he could barely believe that this incontinent and immobile creature was the same daughter that had run lithely across the playground to meet him, chattering with delight about her day at school. He reached for her hand and flinched at the coldness of it; it was more like a claw, with its wrinkled papery skin and bony knuckles. She hadn't moved that hand for two years, even though he spent an hour every day doing vigorous physical therapy to try to stimulate her still body to react. He would stay with her until she awoke and comfort her while she desperately tried to move, her body momentarily forgetting that she was paralysed and panicking at the lack of response from her wasted muscles. He would then administer her dose of morphine and leave her to doze while he prepared breakfast and her prescribed cocktail of drugs, then tear off another page of the calendar and feel the familiar sick feeling in the pit of his stomach as he remembered that today was one day closer to his great fear. In twenty days' time she would turn sixteen, and only he knew how dreadful that was.

'Mum, come in. It's great to see you.' He had forgotten that his mother was coming for the day, but seeing her with her arms full of jars of homemade chutneys and tins of cakes and puddings brought a happy tear to his eye. 'Cup of tea?'

'That would be lovely,' she replied while searching through the fridge. 'Not much food here, my boy, and microwave meals! I can't do with my little boy eating that kind of processed junk. Did you know that there are four tablespoons of sugar in this can? Yes, it's called "hidden sugar". Not the kind of thing you want in your delicate digestive system. I'm sure I've mentioned this kind of thing before.'

'Yes Mother, many a time,' Paul said, chuckling at the way she pronounced 'hidden sugar' as though it were some kind of ferocious African tribesman. 'And I'm due to go shopping tomorrow.'

'I wish you'd let me do that. I do hate you leaving

Katy alone. Where is my granddaughter, by the way?'

'She's having her morning nap, and quite frankly Mother, I don't think she even knows that I'm here at all,' he sighed.

'Oh, don't talk like that. You're the one thing that keeps her alive. She couldn't possibly cope without you. You are a very good father, and don't you dare think anything otherwise,' she said matter of factly as she bustled off towards the bedroom.

But Paul was not so easily consoled. After all, he had driven the car off the road. And there wasn't much to be said for keeping her alive because all but her mind was dead anyway, and that was like a beautiful butterfly flapping its delicate wings against the harsh snare that threatened to close on it at any time. And he knew that time would come. He poured the tea and followed his mother.

Why does nobody come? I've been lying in the dark for so long now, and I'm so cold. I don't know what's wrong with me. I cannot move. I dare not open my eyes again, yet my senses are distorted by inky blackness, which I know is not the night. No twilight could ever be this bleak and starless. Will I ever open my eyes again? Am I alive or is this the murky journey to another world? I am crying, but I cannot feel my tears.

'Katy, Katy, it's Granny here. I've brought your favourite cake today. I know how useless your daddy is at cooking – I've seen his fridge! There's some chocs as well from your grandad. Can't have you wasting away now, can we? I've got so much to tell you. You'll never guess what your Aunt Meredith has done now! But you have a nice sleep and I'll talk to you later.'

She stood up awkwardly and turned to see Paul framed in the doorway. 'Do you think she can hear me?' she asked, with a slight break in her voice.

'Who knows? These drugs are so strong that I'm never entirely sure, but I like to think that she can hear us. She smiles sometimes and once I thought she tried to laugh, but that could be me imagining things of course. Oh, I miss her, and her mother.'

'I know you do, we all do. But we have to be strong for her sake. She's got her whole life ahead of her. Now, where's that tea?' she said, brushing a tear from her eye as she left the room. Paul stood looking at his daughter for another minute, and it was then that he decided, finally, to keep his terrible promise to her.

'Not long now, sweetie, not long.'

He swilled the whisky around the base of the glass and took another sip. He glanced at the calendar. Ten days. He stood up suddenly and strode to Katy's room where she lay as she always did, staring at the ceiling with listless eyes. Those eyes were one of the saddest things, for they had been a vibrant green before and had flashed and sparkled with happiness and humour when she smiled. He was reminded of a quote from Macbeth: 'You see her eyes are open, but their sense is shut.' How true that was of the form that lay before him. He laughed drunkenly at the irony of that particular passage coming back to him after all those years. His hysterical laughter rose to a shrill pitch and then a sob caught in his throat and he fell to his knees, weeping uncontrollably. He rolled over and pulled his knees to his chest and cried for all he was worth, until he drifted into a fitful sleep.

Someone's crying. I can hear the wretched sobs, but I don't know where they are coming from. It feels like far away, in a distant land almost, carried by a cruel wind. I have been abandoned, I feel sure of it. I have been dumped and left to die alone. I am returning to my maker, but my body refuses to let go of this world and so I am torn. I have been drifting like refuse in a stagnant canal and I cannot sink. I don't recognise the hand that feeds me and lifts me from my warm resting place and yet I know I should. I am paying a debt that was meant for someone else. Please God, take me.

Paul held the crumpled piece of paper in his hand as he sat by Katy's bed waiting to comfort her when she woke from whatever demons had plagued her beautiful mind during the night. He read it again and again, although he knew the words off by heart and was familiar with every childish curl and feminine flourish that graced the pale pink page. It was an odd colour to choose for such a sombre piece of prose, but it reflected the blithe happiness of his daughter as she wrote these final wishes. He had kept it in a drawer next to his bed ever since he had found it when he was sorting through her things after the crash. It had caused him equal amounts of hope and anguish over the last two years. It stated the normal things that you would expect to find in a teenager's will – that she wanted all her money to go to the RSPCA and her clothes and stuffed toys to Oxfam. It read that she wanted the church to be adorned in red roses at her funeral and that she wanted to be buried next to her family. And then came the extract that had caused such a surge of emotions in Paul's heart:

'If before adulthood I am ever left in a state where I am physically or mentally dependent on a person or machine and have no apparent will to live, then I wish to be allowed to die on the eve of my sixteenth birthday. I could not face losing my dignity as I progress into adulthood, and I trust that my beloved family will have done all that can be done. I have no wish to spend my life in a wheelchair and I would not want to bestow upon anybody the duty of looking after me in an impaired state. I would die with a wonderful childhood behind me and no painful struggle ahead of me.'

He read it one last time and felt a great warmth flooding through his body. His heart was brimming with love for his only child and he offered up a quick prayer asking forgiveness for what he was about to do. He filled the syringe with morphine and slid it into Katy's arm as he had done so many times before. He gently kissed her forehead and pushed the syringe.

'Goodbye, Kate. Rest in peace, my love.'

He then filled the syringe once more and pressed it through his own skin. He flinched slightly and then lay down beside Katy, who had never awoken from the nightmare. This time it would have an end, it would all come to an end.

I open my eyes and someone is there, someone I once knew a long time ago. And the stars are bright around me as I am lifted from my cramped position. What is he saying? It sounds painfully like goodbye, like he is leaving me again. How can this be? And then I know, a deep memory stirs inside me and a great sadness wells up. He has made the final sacrifice for me. He cannot tread the turf of Our Father for he has committed a crime of a magnitude that forbids him to pass through the golden gates. The fiery blade of love is double-edged and even the strongest may fall, but he falls with a grace and purpose, and carries with him the weight of my eternal love.

Katrina's Vampire

Leanne Rutter

Katrina's Vampire

Katrina

Cold. Dark. It's all around, it's everywhere. Smothering darkness, twisting my insides with fear, making my mind run riot with images of vampires and werewolves and witches and other shady creatures of the night. I could have mistaken them for a shadow . . . or they could be following me, tracing my every step, ready to pounce . . . but when I look around, there's nothing to be seen but the dotted streetlights, setting an odd orange glow on the slippery pavement. It's all in my head, I know it is, but as I walk on, I hear footsteps . . . vampires following me, wanting to kill me, leave me as just a bloodless corpse.

Agh. I'm letting my imagination run off again. No such thing, no such thing. There are no vampires, no creatures of darkness; nothing is out to get you . . . but those footsteps. I pirouette again, an agile spin on the damp floor, sodden with leaves. No one is there. Why do I feel that someone is following me? Why do I feel so afraid? I've walked these streets in the darkness all my life and this never happened. What's changed? Why does it seem like suddenly a sixth sense is trying to warn me of something that isn't there? Something that sets every tiny hair on my body on end. This is madness. Home now. As I go to open the front door, I can't help it; I turn around and stare, wide-eyed, and check, before thrusting the key into the lock and scurrying inside where I double lock the door. I'm safe. I'm OK. Relief floods through me as I sit on the bottom step of the stairs. I'm home. I'm fine. Nothing can get me here. Maybe I should put some crosses up . . . just in case.

Her 'Vampire'

I watched her walking home today. I followed her all the way, my mind photographing her every move. She is so . . . intriguing. I stayed behind her all the way to her house. Of course I knew where she lived already; I've know that since almost the beginning. She looked so nervy as she walked. She kept turning round and staring down the street as if she knew someone was following her. But how could she? I'm ever so good at keeping myself hidden, keeping myself as a shadow.

Her long black hair was loose today. It falls almost to her waist now. Black and silky. I'd like to stroke it. It was flickering behind her, enticing me, asking me to touch it. I would have liked to. I have a piece of her hair, a perfect black lock. I stood outside the hair-dresser's when she was having her hair cut a few months back. I ran in once she had left and took a piece off the floor before the man could sweep up. I'm glad it's so long again, though. It could be dangerous, if you think about it. Hair that long . . . she could hang herself with it. I stood outside her house for about half an hour after she'd closed the door. I caught glimpses of her silhouette a few times in the windows, when she pulled the downstairs curtains, when she walked past the upstairs window. And every glimpse I treasure, like every picture of her I own. I wish I could be there now, a fly on the wall perhaps, or, maybe a cat . . . that she loved and gave lots of attention. Being loved and stroked in that tall, narrow house, just outside of Camden Town.

Katrina

A new day. It will be good this time. I will not be made to jump by the sound of nothingness, or the sight of nothingness. I will not let my senses trick me, telling me to be scared when there is no need. Or at least, I'll try not to. It's so, so hard, though. But still, a new day.

As I shower and the hot water splatters all over me, on my skin, my hair sticking to my back, almost to my waist, all my worries seem to be washed away, down the plughole. Soft warm towels sooth my pale skin, soaking up the droplets that cling on like tiny sparking diamonds. Hair all around my shoulders, towel-dried and rough, tangled, falling down over my chest, over the towel that's hanging damply against my ribs, heavy strands gently hitting me through the thick towel as I walk to my room.

There I pick out my clothes and start dressing. I don't want to be dressed in dark colours as I usually am, but I feel I need it. The black remains – all black except for the pink beads at my throat and wrists and the pink stripes against my legs. As I look at myself in the mirror, I think that perhaps today I should be bright; dress in bright denim and pink, lime green cords, or a purple coat or anything. Not black, because black attracts the vampires and they will haunt me again. But I don't change a thing. I pick up my bag and walk out of the house.

The day is bright and crisp. Blue, blue sky, making the world bright and happier. Orange and red leaves scattered on the ground. Bright faces, with bright eyes, green and blue. Bright lips, pinks and reds. All is good and colourful today. Never mind if I'm not, all else is and that will rub off on me. No vampires today. They'll keep away. They will not haunt me and chase me and run around within my skull. Not today they won't. The day is too happy, too bright. All will be well today. I arrive at work and walk in.

Her 'Vampire'

By the time she came out this morning I had been waiting at least twenty minutes. I didn't want to miss her. I wanted to see her as she took her first step out of the house.

Her hair looks beautiful; it's shimmering in the sunlight, all clean and soft, bouncing loosely against her back. It's entrancing . . . she's entrancing. And soon she will notice me, very soon. I follow her to work; she doesn't seem so nervy this morning. She's holding her head up high. Her flawless pale skin contrasts with her dark hair and eyes and clothes. She seems deep in thought, but happier all the same. Her lips, her gorgeous, luscious lips curve into a smile, directed several times at people that obviously don't know her. She smiles at the sky and at the ground as well, then looks thoughtful, then sees someone and smiles at them too. If only she would smile at me. But I am just a shadow, just a shadow, always watching her.

Katrina

Work has been good and easy today. Quite a few people come into the shop this morning, asking about rare records and albums. I work in a little bootleg music shop, which is under another shop in

Camden High Street. A lot of people come and see us, browse for hours on end while music blasts, music I choose. I chatter with customers and they buy CDs by bands that no one's heard of, or whose members are dead, or who will never play again.

The morning passes and no thoughts of vampires flitter through my brain. Not a ghoul nor a werewolf dares trespass. I feel safe again. I walk down the high street and into the market, weaving through the bustling crowd. I get myself lunch and sit with a few friends . . . and it's then, then that I get that feeling again, just as I'm biting into my kebab. I get the feeling I'm being watched. My eyes search the crowds. Anyone of them could be my vampire, anyone. I try to ignore it, but I can't.

After eating, I leave my friends and wander around awhile, but I feel nervous. Brightness, come back. Make me happy and carefree again. Shine into my head and scare the dark beings away. I stare at the ground as I walk along, not wanting to see all the people, with any one of them possibly out to get me. I walk straight into something and my head shoots up so quickly I could give myself whiplash. My eyes widen in a second and a loud gasp escapes my lips. A man is looking at me. He has large blue eyes; his hair is a deep blue. His head is tilted to the side and he is looking at me apologetically as he mutters his sorrys. Not a vampire. Just a man, someone I bumped into. A normal person.

The market is too crowded; I need the safety of the shop. I hurry back as quickly as I can.

Her 'Vampire'

Once I'd seen her off I went to work myself. I work in HMV, one of the big record stores, not like hers. The pay is better for me, but working beside her in that tiny shop all day would be heaven.

As soon as my lunch break hits I rush all the way up the high street to the market, down all the steps, almost tripping as I do so, and then I see her. She's sitting at a table with two men and a girl. I stand and watch her. I hate those people sitting around her. It should be me. They shouldn't be there. They deserve to die. And then she goes all weird, looking around, staring wildly for a few seconds, and when she goes back to her food, she's all tense. She doesn't see me, how could she? She doesn't know it's me. She shouldn't know that it's anyone. Maybe she feels it. Deep within her, maybe she knows.

After she leaves, I look around the market for a short while. I don't buy anything, just look, with images of me gently twisting her hair round my finger in my head. And then, there she is, head down, looking forlorn and scared. And it's so easy; I just go up to her and bump into her, straight on. She looks at me in shock, in horror, gasping, her eyes, deep, dark pools in her perfectly white face, her long hair swishing a little as she looks up at me sharply. And I smile at her, what I hope is a comforting smile, and quietly apologise for bumping into her. She nods slightly then scurries off. That is the best thing that has happened to me in months.

Katrina

The afternoon is tedious, and yet, the darkness is coming, and it terrifies me. I have that long walk in the darkness, and I'm so scared. How I wish I could stay here, just sleep here tonight. I don't know what is going on, but I've had this quiet, niggling, terrifying feeling for weeks now, months, and it's not going away. Instead it's just getting worse and worse. It can't be wrong, I can't be wrong. My vampires are starting to wake up, getting ready to pounce as the sun goes down. I can't go home tonight. Not tonight. I'm just so scared. I need someone there with me.

I'll go home with a friend – that's what I'll do. Sleep on someone's couch. It'll be fine, and tomorrow I have the afternoon off so I'll be able to walk back in the light and all will be well and good again. It will.

At the end of work I rush out. I run through the

market, past all the food stalls and under the bridge to The Black Rose, a beautiful shop where my friend Dani works. He is just closing up. I grab his arm, maybe a little too roughly, and I look at him. And I can't help it, I burst into tears. Then I feel all is OK, and he takes me home. I sleep on the sofa, all safe and warm, wrapped in a blanket.

Her 'Vampire'

My work finished earlier than hers by a little so I ran up the high street and waited outside her shop to see her. Maybe today I could talk to her. Today has already been a good day. She saw me, looked right at me, noticed me for the very first time. I will dream about that moment. I build myself up, I really am going to speak to her, I will, I know it. When she comes out, she's running, and runs all the way to the market. I follow her as quickly as possible without letting her notice me. She stops outside a shop, where a man is locking up and they hug; he envelops her in his strong, skinny arms and I hate him. My insides are burning. I could breathe fire on him. I'm going mad. How dare he? How dare he touch her? And her, how can she let him? I feel sick with jealousy and hatred. Then as she walks with him, I follow, becoming a shadow again, my eyes gleaming angrily. And then, her final crime, she goes into his house with him. I sit down on a bench across the road. I sit there for hours to see if she comes out. But she doesn't. She stays the night. The whole night. It's more than I can take.

Katrina

I go to work the next day and I feel happy and confident again. The day passes quickly and instead of scurrying home after work, I wander around the market. I have nothing to be scared of. No one is out to get me, no one at all. I'm fine, I'm well and happy and safe, and conscious of it. It is a little dark as I walk home, but no vampires are following me tonight. As I get to my front door, I don't look around as I usually do. I just get my keys out and open the door. The next thing I know, I'm on the floor, my nose pressed against the carpet. My back hurts where the intruder pushed me, my head hurts, having being knocked against the floor. This is it. My vampire exists. He's in my house, standing behind me. I'm going to die. He's going to kill me or hurt me or take me far from here, to places I don't want to be.

He lifts me, with surprising gentleness, and carries me up the stairs and into my room, placing me on my chair, and binding my hands and feet. There are tears in my eyes and my breath is short. What's going to happen to me? What will he do? Then I see him for the first time and I let out a little shriek of surprise and terror rolled into one. Large blue eyes look at me, a face topped with deep blue hair. Oh, God. Oh, God. This is the end, isn't it? No strange sense of calm passes through me, just the sadness that my life is going to end, and the fear of pain. Oh, God. I let loose, and the tears stream down my face.

Her 'Vampire'

When I see her the next day, I follow her to the shop. I skipped work. I'm a total mess. Then I walk to her house. Before she even leaves work I walk to her house and sit in the bushes by her door and wait. She takes ages, hours; I sit, I wait. What else is there for me to do? There is nothing, nothing at all.

Eventually she comes home and unlocks the door. I stand up and push her inside, knocking her to the floor, then go in after her and lock the door behind me. I'm in her tall and narrow house, but no, I'm no fly on the wall, and no, I'm no cat she loves. I'm someone she fears, but not for much longer, not much longer at all. I carry her up her own stairs and into her own room and sit her in her own chair. She barely struggles, she seems dazed, but I know her heart is beating fast, I know that her whole body is shaking in pure terror. I sit her on her chair, and tie her hands and feet. Then she stares at me and gasps so loudly. She recognises me from yesterday. And I smile; I sit on the edge of her bed and smile at her. Then slowly I get up, walk behind her and stroke her silky soft hair. And I tell her about the months and months of wanting her, seeing her every day, following her, working out her daily routine. Her eyes seem to get larger and larger against her stunned, pale face. Her breathing is fast and shaky, there are tears rolling down her face, and she keeps blinking. Slight sobbing noises are let out every now and again, though she almost tries to hide it. Then I tell her of the hatred and the jealousy. And as I do it, I take her hair and twist it, as if a rope. It's strong and thick. Slowly I wrap it around her neck and she becomes almost hysterical. Her body shakes like mad, she cries bitterly, tears falling off her jaw and on to her chest, her eyes squeezed shut. It's the end for you, my dear. You will die at a tender age, all because of me. I pull her hair tight around her throat, until not a breath is left in her body, until she is still. It is done. Months of this . . . this obsession is over. Gone in an instant. I look at her throat. It's red, raw. Her face is deathly pale, her eyes wide open now, glazed. I smile at her, nicely. I get some scissors, and cut off the silky, ebony hair, tying it with her pink and black tights. It's mine now. She will always be with me. Forever.

I leave the house, and I never come back.

The Red Jacket

Laura Tobia

The Red Jacket

The bus jolted violently as it collided with the dazed kangaroo. It had just turned midnight and the Japanese tourists on the luxury coach were hysterical. Many were excited at having seen the very first Australian animal on their holiday. Others were quietly crying, deeply distressed by the fact that they were responsible for the death of a kangaroo on their first evening in the outback. They hadn't even reached their destination.

The driver had done his best to avoid the inevitable, but unfortunately had just seconds to brake and try to swerve out of the way. The kangaroo had stopped in the middle of the road, apparently hypnotised by the headlights of the oncoming vehicle. After several minutes of mayhem on the bus, a middle-aged, slightly plump man, wearing a bold red coat announced that he wanted to get a closer look at the kangaroo. The driver suggested that this would be the only opportunity that they would get to stand so close to a wild animal. He encouraged them to go and take a closer look. First off the bus was the man with the red jacket and with his camera ready and a smile he was soon engulfed in darkness. After a little persuasion, many others in the party decided that they wanted a closer look and joined him.

Three of the strongest in the group struggled to lift up the kangaroo and rest it against the door of the bus. It looked as though it was in a very deep sleep, as if it hadn't been injured at all. The man with the red coat requested a photograph with the animal and the driver obliged. Flashes were soon illuminating the night, but it took much longer than expected for all the members of the party to be photographed alongside the kangaroo. For any onlookers, it would have been quite an amusing situation to observe. However, as it was around one o'clock in the morning and in the middle of nowhere, there where no witnesses.

Just as the people were returning to their seats on the tour bus, the red-jacketed man decided to go one step further. He placed his coat around the shoulders of the kangaroo and pushed its two front paws into the sleeves. He asked the driver to take another picture as he posed alongside with a childish grin stretching from ear to ear. The camera flashed brightly, and at that precise instant the kangaroo awoke. For a moment it looked startled and scared, but then the kangaroo bounded off into the distance. The tourist looked absolutely petrified. The driver appeared thoughtful but said nothing.

The man to whom the red jacket belonged was in

deep shock (thus not really in a position to judge), but he would have bet money that the kangaroo had winked at him before it leaped elegantly into the darkness that surrounded them. Ironically, the man had no money to make a bet, as it had been carried away by the 'dead' kangaroo. Not only his wallet, but his credit cards and traveller's cheques had all disappeared into the bush with the kangaroo.

As they discussed the event in bemusement, the tourists could find no logical explanation for what had just unfolded. Every theory suggested was wilder and more extravagant than the preceding one.

* * *

Too humiliated to report the incident and too ashamed of their own stupidity, the tour group had abruptly left Australia and returned home to Japan on the next available flight. However, the incident was reported in the local press, and the story was recounted throughout the community with huge amusement.

A little after the publicity had died down, I happened to be waiting for a friend at a bar in town, close to where the incident took place. It was a typical outback pub and, as usual, there was a group of rowdy men with large beer bellies, drinking several beers each. Although I was minding my own business, I couldn't help overhearing their conversation. Amid lots of laughter, one member of the group was bragging about how he had taught his pet kangaroo to perform tricks. He was explaining that whenever he had any guests, the kangaroo would take their coats and hang them up.

As I watched from the other end of the bar, I could not help noticing that the man who owned the pet kangaroo was buying all the drinks. As he pulled out a big wad of notes from his pocket to buy yet another round for his friends, the barman turned and asked if he had won the lottery. He winked and replied, 'Yes, but I didn't have to buy a ticket!'

By this time I had become quite engrossed, and hoped that my friend would not arrive until my curiosity had been satisfied. Gradually, it became apparent, by comments made by the group, that the man drove for a living.

After a few more beers, the man announced that he had to leave. I was somewhat annoyed to hear this, as I hadn't discovered how the man had obtained the money. I just wanted another few minutes to see if I could piece this jigsaw puzzle together. My friend was over half an hour late, but I hadn't even noticed.

The man made his exit, saying that he was due at the airport early the next morning. After he said this, he commented that he had to 'pick up another bunch of suckers'. There was a loud roar of laughter and he got up and made his way precariously towards the door. It was obvious that he'd had too much to drink that night.

On his way out he paused briefly to pick up a smart red jacket and throw it on over his shoulders. As he staggered out of the bar, laughing to himself, it was evident that the coat was several sizes too small.

A Dog-Chewed Ball

Abbie Todd

A Dog-Chewed Ball

'I . . . am . . . Aimee.' That's three words. Three words I can't even say. The message shoots from my brain to my mouth, and I'm thinking, 'Go on, say it, say it,' so I open my mouth and a series of random sounds fall out untidily, like a cupboard just waiting to throw out its contents as soon as someone opens the door. Like the objects that fall out – a dusty book, an old table tennis bat, a dog-chewed ball – I make no sense. I can communicate about as much as that deflated, hole-ridden ball, lying on the floor, and I am about as much use.

I am aware that I sound self-pitying. I can't help it. It is because I can't make myself heard, and *they* certainly don't understand me. They are all the same anyway. Well, by that I mean that they all wear white coats. I've given up trying to distinguish between their tight faces, with their sharp, intellectual expressions. My brain finds it hard enough to keep me from dribbling all over my pristine pillow, let alone remember faces. That's all except one. Janet, I think her name is, or Julie. I have a feeling I am her favourite. She visits me almost every day. She always looks tired, bags hanging under her eyes like the ones a donkey carries, but then she makes a

117

special effort to smile, and I make a special effort to smile back. Only I don't. Well, at least I think I don't. I can feel my face contort, and as she articulates a sigh of sympathy, I think about how ugly I must look.

She brushes my hair for me. My hair is dull. It is the colour of tree bark, and about twice as brittle. It is short. Sometimes I manage to move a little, or a breeze will catch it, and it will fall across my eye, and I will have to blink and blink to try and get it out. All I can do is sit there in discomfort until someone (usually her) comes and brushes it away. Even though my hair is dull, and like tree bark, she makes it feel like a beautiful, golden mane, like the perfection you see only on a Disney film. The way she strokes it, and arranges it just right around my face, I could be Rapunzel, or Melisande. Remember her? The one whose hair just grew and grew. I watch Julie's quick hand movements as she tucks the blanket under me, and fluffs the pillow in that pointless way nurses always do. I envy her deftness and co-ordination.

Paralysis is a word that I think about a lot. Well, that, and *him*. If you can imagine that I'm reading this, by the way, think of my voice as saying '*him*' with all the venom that I can possibly muster. I am here, like this, because of *him*. He is, or was, my father, and he killed my mother, and left me like this.

A Dog-Chewed Ball

At first I couldn't believe those words that were rolling around my head, like a solitary sock in a tumble dryer: 'He killed my mum, he did this to me . . . He killed my mum, he did this to me . . .' but when you've heard them in your head as many times as I have, then you begin to accept them as reality, not fiction.

In the beginning I convinced myself that I would be OK. Well, obviously I knew I wouldn't be, but the pain was lessened by the ridiculous thought that my mum was somehow still alive. Stupid really, considering I'd heard the crack . . . the crack. If I could shudder I would! Anyway, I imagined how she'd come flying through the door, after being in a coma for several weeks, relieved to see me alive at least, take me in her arms, tell me I'd be fine, that she loved me, and that they'd arrested *him*.

That fantasy lasted for about two weeks. Then I got my first real visitor. I knew it wasn't one of the white coat people. They never knock. This one knocked, softly and quickly, as if they were in a hurry to get in, or get away again. The door opened enough to let the noises of the hospital drift through, and I lay there thinking, 'Is it Mum or Dad . . . Mum or Dad?' and the sock in the tumble dryer started up again: 'Mum or Dad . . . Mum or Dad . . . Mum or Dad?' I couldn't move to see, so I strained my eyes as far round as they would go. It hurt.

The sock moved into my stomach and then my heart started pumping fast. I saw a pair of shoes. Men's shoes. Then a face, looming over me, peering into my eyes, at my unresponsive expression. Then I was mad. Really, really mad, because I knew, and he was standing over me, breathing his horrible coffee-infused breath all over me, and I knew that there was nothing I could do about it. I wanted to tell him how mad I was. I wanted to roar like the revving engine of an old car, pound my fists against his chest so hard that I would break him, like he had broken me. I wanted to shout, 'Over here! He did it!' but all I could do was grunt pathetically, dribble a little, and flare my nostrils angrily.

He didn't say anything on that first visit. He seemed emotional, like he couldn't speak because he couldn't find the words. I knew how he felt. After he'd gone, the sock moved back into my head, and the same realisation bumped around again and again and again. An epiphany. I was stuck like this. My mum was dead. Then the leaking started: all down my cheeks, over the pristine pillow, and in my hair. I think it even got as far as the top of my nightdress. As I bawled to myself, rivers of snot streamed down my face, and I couldn't even raise a hand to wipe them off. Disgusting.

And then suddenly there was an image printed on the sock: a small, uninteresting girl in a school uniform opening the front door to her house, and peering in. The image expanded to fill my head, and then it was a moving picture, and it had full surround sound, and there was shouting. My parents. I couldn't tell what they were saying – the words blurred into a long stream of abuse, anger, and pure venom. I knew whatever they were hurling at each other was absolutely vile, and I knew that I was not supposed to hear. That suited me. I didn't even want to hear. I slammed the door in the hope that they would hear me and stop fighting, but they carried on regardless. I could smell that dinner was burning, and went into the kitchen, rapidly filling with smoke, took the pan off the hob, opened a window, and turned the TV on, loud.

As the smoke drifted towards the hallway, a draft of air caught it, and wafted it upwards into the filter of the smoke alarm. It went off: *'bleep, bleep, bleep, bleep, bleep . . .'* It was so deafening, confusing, and the smell of smoke was catching in my throat and making me cough. Still the TV blared away: spouting out nonsense, filling my head with disorder, and still the smoke alarm continued to bleep. Something from this cacophony of sound was missing, though. Then I realised they had stopped. They had heard it, and they were listening.

Mum cursed. 'I forgot I'd put the dinner on.'

He called her an idiot. 'Now look what you've done!'

I heard footsteps on the stairs, and still that incessant bleeping went on. I took a magazine from the table, intending to waft the smoke away myself.

'I'll get it!' I yelled, walking through into the hall, but Mum was already poised at the top of the stairs. She hadn't noticed me, and over the continual bleeping, I was sure that they hadn't heard me. But I could hear them, hear exactly what they were saying.

'Where do you think you're going?'

'Don't be ridiculous, Jeff. I can't just leave it to go off.'

'I'll get it!' I said again, but still they didn't hear, didn't want to hear.

'We've not finished discussing this yet,' he shouted.

She laughed at him, and turned. 'We're not discussing anything, Jeff, we're just fighting,' and he spun her around to face him. Roughly. Too roughly. By that time I was at the bottom of the stairs, ready to tell them I'd stop the smoke alarm, ready to stop them arguing. I could see his face, so angry, just as I could see her foot slip from the stair behind, and fall.

Did he push her? I don't know. I was watching her foot, not his hand. You want my opinion? Damn right, he did, and I know why. Money. That was probably what they'd been arguing about. I always knew we were well off, though they were never extravagant with it. I think they were saving it, for me to go to college or something. At least, she was. *He* wanted to spend it, *he* had other plans. Well actually, I don't think that is fair. I don't think he planned to do it at all. I'm not even sure if he consciously did do it. I do think that it must have been in his head all the time, like my sock, the amount of money she had, the amount of money he could have been spending, that new car he really wanted, that she just wouldn't let him have. I think that it was a split-second of misjudgement.

Anyway, I rushed up towards my mum, falling, to try and catch her, break her fall – anything – and his glazed eyes turned to me. He shouted a warning, and her body hit me like a spoonful of sugar being dropped into a cup of tea. Just like the sugar, we seemed to dissolve into the floor below in a mass of broken bones and blood. I was underneath her; I had broken her fall, yet somehow . . . somehow her head had hit the hard, polished, wooden floor (*his* idea.) Somehow, it had managed to make the kind of crack you'd expect to hear coming from a building site, not a person. Somehow, my eyes managed to remain focused on his distorted face for a few seconds before I lost consciousness. That face, leering over me, with his coffee-infused breath, pain running along its lines like a train on a railway.

That day he came in, that was when I realised what he must have told them: 'It was an accident.

We were arguing. The smoke alarm was going. She went to turn it off and she fell.' Of course they would have believed him. He would have been distraught, and they would have sympathised, because he had just lost a daughter and a wife in one day. Yes, he would have been distraught. He did love us. He had never been a bad father, and we were just a normal family really, and it was just a normal fight. It's just that he went too far.

I am sure they will want to turn me off soon. This machine that keeps me alive bleeps in my ear all day, and I cannot escape the memory of that smoke alarm going off: *'bleep, bleep, bleep . . .'* and I cannot forget what he did. Maybe in between them turning off the machine and me dying, maybe when I will no longer have to hear that constant bleeping, I will be able to forgive him. But not before then.

He hadn't planned it, but he had achieved the perfect crime, really. No evidence, no witnesses. Well, only me, and I am about as useful as a dog-chewed ball, remember?

Crime of an Innocent Mind

Gemma Tomkys

Crime of an Innocent Mind

It was shocking news – the type of news that you spend half your life dreading and the next half mourning. However, it is inevitable that at some time in your short life you will be dragged out naked, thrown into the harsh light of day and forced to face the information that is being thrust in front of your eyes, whether you desire it or not. It is inevitable that one day you will have to deal with it, but it is the way in which you deal with it that is the test, the challenge that you must overcome. The way in which you deal with the news measures your strength of character and strength of mind.

Timothy, however, was frankly in no state of mind to handle the news, let alone deal with it. Nor were the remaining members of class S8 at Summer Field School and nor was young Miss Write a willing messenger, but someone had to tell them. There had been an accident. That was easy enough to say, but seeing the faces of the innocent children sitting in front of her, thinking they were old enough to handle anything when they were so obviously not, made it difficult for Miss Write to continue. How do you tell twenty-eight eleven-year-olds that a fellow pupil had died in an accident only four hours ago? It was a difficult one. Miss Write pondered the possibility of waiting until they noticed he was missing, but it was absurd. It would be all over the papers, *'Young Boy Killed in Hit and Run'* and Matthew had been the loudest, the funniest and most popular kid in class.

She gathered her wits about her and began to speak in the sweet, soft voice that the children had known only to bring them glad tidings. Gradually, she broke the news to them, explaining that he hadn't looked, explaining how the car had come out of nowhere and how there was nothing that the doctors could have done to save him. She left out the details, how his body had been thrown several feet before crashing to the ground. She decided not to explain that the unidentified driver simply left a little boy to suffocate to death on the sidewalk with a collapsing lung. After all, there was only so much she could do and only so much they could take.

It was already too much. The salty tears of the children poured in bucketloads down their pale faces. The classroom, normally filled with laughter, echoed with the devastated sobs of children who simply did not understand and didn't particularly want to. To understand would be to accept, and to accept would mean to forget, and to forget Matthew would mean doing him the biggest injustice that they were capable of committing. Yet throughout this outcry, one boy sat silent. One boy just stared into the space that rudely separated him from the distant boundaries of alternate dimensions. He didn't want to be there; in fact, there was the last place he wanted to be, because there he had heard the worst possible news that his ears would ever bear witness too. He was upset, just like the others, but sadness was not the only emotion Timothy was experiencing.

* * *

Walking down the corridor of Summer Field was not an experience he would wish to repeat. It felt like walking through a morgue when you weren't supposed to be there. It felt like intruding on some morbid, corrupt affair. And when everyone turned to watch, the simple task became intolerable. Cold, convicting eyes were everywhere Timothy looked, and the word 'guilty' was being uttered by untrusting tongues everywhere. He kept his head down and fixed his eyes on the floor, but when that too turned to blood, it all became too much. He screamed.

'Timothy?'

He stirred.

'Timothy, if you don't get your bottom out of bed immediately, you will be walking to school!'

Opening his eyes, for a few glorious moments, Timothy thought that it had all been just a dream. He jumped out of bed, overjoyed by the feeling of freedom that flowed through his veins and ran downstairs, overcome by relief, burst through the kitchen door, little short of ecstatic, and stopped dead. The paper was on the kitchen table. *'Young Boy Killed in Hit and Run.'* It took a few heart-rending moments for Timothy to realise that it was all far from a dream and far too close to reality.

The paper was close, only steps away, but Timothy wasn't sure he wanted to read it. After all what could it tell him that he didn't already know? That the killer was a young boy? A boy who was just 'mucking around'? No, he already knew all that, and more.

The police came into school the following week with the news that they were doing more to inform students on road safety, that they were doing more to ensure that this type of thing didn't happen again. But Timothy was fed up with people wanting to do more. He'd had enough of people reassuring him that the pain would go away soon. He wasn't stupid; he knew that he would have to live with this for the rest of his life, carry it around on his shoulders for as many wretched days as this life chose to inflict on him. And what did they know about it anyway? Nothing. Nothing at all.

That night Timothy sat up in bed, thinking. He was numb and nothing could distract him from his present melancholic state. No one seemed to understand it either. His parents adopted a cocktail emotion of anxiety mixed with confusion, yet still had the cheek to say, 'We understand.' They didn't, but no one could really condemn them for their naivety. Tears were what were expected from an eleven-year-old who'd just lost a best mate. Theoretical questions about life and death were forecasted for later, and the end result would be wisdom gained. But these attempts at calculating life and grief are flawed. They do not consider the possibility of human individuality, which, although rapidly being consumed by conformity, has not been completely overcome yet.

As the next few days progressed, so did the story of Matthew Harper's death. Soon, the information once known only to a privileged few was offered to all. The whole of England was 'affected' by his death and 'appalled' by the issues that it raised. The death of Matthew Harper was discussed in every household in every neighbourhood, and used by every man and charity that could benefit from its profile. This did not do Matthew's parents any good. They were the close-knit, religious, quiet-life type of family, who wanted to mourn the death of their only son in peace without being hounded by the press to express their grief publicly. Nor did it help Timothy. His mind was in a constant state of chaos, thoughts and grievances being thrown in all directions. Yet with a story like this, the emotions of those actually involved are often forgotten, merely shoved out of the way for convenience, or taken and exploited by the press. For to show *true* grief, to show how lives have been ripped apart, would divert attention from the story itself. The horror experienced by those close to it is punishment for something society has done. However, it is not the close ones who should be punished; they are the innocent bystanders. Most of the time.

'Oh, how you've grown! You were only this high when I was here last time,' his Grandma wailed, indicating a height that would not do justice to a mouse. She said that every time. Probably every grandma said it every time. There was probably some secret handbook that instructed them to say it every time. *Potter's Guide to Being the Perfect Grandma*. It's potty all right. What nutter could possibly come to the conclusion that this phrase would make the grandchildren glad to see them? Quite the contrary.

Timothy's mother must have been potty too if she thought that a visit from his grandparents was going to help in any way at all. However, being the obliging son and grandson he had always been, Timothy decided to play along with this act of normality. Yet this calm condition was soon invaded by guilt and within a matter of days, Timothy had changed from being an obedient son to a secretive and detached child from hell.

It had been ten days since the accident when Randall received a memo informing him of an emergency meeting, to take place at Wafeside police station. Randall had been on the force for nearly fifteen years and had kids of his own and this Harper case disturbed him. It was bad enough when an adult kills a child but when a child takes a life of another child, the crime reaches a totally different level of immorality. Our children are the next generation, and if they become capable of such inhumane acts so young, what hope does humankind have for the future? The answer: very little.

However, it seemed that the investigation had been stepped up a little. The reaction of the press and the public required that the police were seen to be doing something. He arrived fifteen minutes late as usual, and was greeted with the oh-so-old comment, 'Better late than never, Randall.' He walked through the door, hands clasped around a cup of coffee, cold before he had a chance to put it to his lips.

'Well, I guess we can make a start, now everyone is here.' Randall hated this. Sergeant Mayard was making a point of the fact that Randall was the last to arrive, as if it wasn't blatantly obvious in the first place. If he was late, he was late; there was no point in rubbing the fact in further. If he was always late, he was always late; they should have picked up on that a long time ago and begun to page the times of meetings fifteen minutes early.

'As you know our major suspect for this inquiry is Timothy Weston.'

Randall did not know this. He had been sent back-up reading, which he was asked to get through before the meeting, but he never bothered with formalities. To him, paperwork was a deterrent rather than an incitement.

'You look confused, Randall.' He was stating the obvious again. Randall was always confused at the beginning.

'Timothy Weston, Randall, was Matthew Harper's best friend.' This case got more sinister every minute. But Randall wasn't simply going to accept the information that was being fed to him right away, unlike the pathetic, brain-dead zombies he was surrounded by.

'And what, pray tell, is your evidence?'

'You obviously haven't done your reading, Randall.' Right again. 'Well, we know that the driver was a young boy because he could not be seen through the window, and I have also discovered that Timothy Weston was missing from gym class at the very time of the accident.' This was deemed as enough evidence to bring Timothy in to question, but Randall wasn't satisfied. There were many holes in the story that needed to be filled. Perhaps the driver was bending down at the time the witness looked up. Perhaps Timothy Weston simply hated gym class. Randall had hated gym himself, as a child.

That Timothy Weston was only a child was a fact very much over-looked by the majority of officers at the station. They seemed to be feeding off this case like hyenas off an antelope, as if they were drug addicts needing an injection of its details every half an hour. They arrested Timothy at his house, while he was watching cartoons. Did it not strike the arresting officers as slightly odd that their murder suspect was entertained by little green men with big heads, and dogs that could fly? It seemed that only Randall could maintain a clear head. He only hoped he had a chance to interview him.

The interview was held as soon as they reached the station and was indeed conducted by Randall. When he entered the room, a surge of desperation clawed at his chest. The boy sitting in front of him was vacant, not a boy at all, simply a collection of bones going through the motions. Randall kept his cool and took his time to reach his seat. The purpose of this was to put his victim's nerves on edge, but Randall doubted whether the silhouette sitting in front of him had any nerves left to unsettle. He took a sip of his cold coffee and prepared himself to speak, but before the words left his mouth, the boy interrupted.

'Look I don't think we need to waste your time or mine here.'

This was not what Randall had expected and he was thrown.

'You're thrown, aren't you?'

The boy was reading his mind and Randall didn't like it. He felt exposed, and found it difficult to compose himself.

'Thought so.' The boy smiled and looked down, generously giving Randall the time he needed to find his feet again. It didn't take long.

'You're right. I'm a busy person and you're a kid . . .'

'A kid on a murder charge?' The laughter that followed unsettled Randall again, so the boy looked at the floor.

'Innocent until proven guilty, remember, but to make it easier for us both, why don't you just tell me what you know?'

'Good idea. I did it.'

Randall was again left speechless.

'I did it, I killed Matthew.'

Silence.

Timothy had to repeat this phrase many times until he was finally taken seriously. The officer in front of him was clearly a pro and Timothy could tell that he normally kept his own feelings out of reach from his work. However, he also guessed that the officer had children of his own and therefore Timothy could comprehend the difficulty he was having accepting what he was being told. Killing a best friend was not on the agenda for normal eleven-year-old boys, but Timothy wasn't normal; he was a freak.

Knowing that you have killed someone isn't easy to come to grips with no matter how the death occurred. The police had seen many types of murderers – brutal gang members, timid but jealous lovers, even innocent – but had never come into contact with an eleven-year-old murderer who did-n't appear to give a damn. The procedures trailed almost effortlessly one after another, yet Timothy had refused to talk in detail on the matter. According to the station, Randall had solved the case; Randall had won, but he didn't feel much like celebrating. He could not close the case in his mind.

The trial was to be the final stage. Timothy found humour in thinking of it as his judgment day. People flocked to the courthouse to quench the thirst of their morbid minds. Loved ones, still unable to understand what was going on around them, came to offer their support, and Randall came not know-ing why. There was a great hush as Timothy was escorted to his box in overalls far too big for him. Adult clothes for an adult crime. And then it all began.

Things did not begin favourably for Timothy. Although his lawyer said nothing, Timothy could tell. His lawyer had little faith in the ending, as the trial was to terminate with Timothy's testimony. And he was right to be doubtful. As predicted, the very first question asked was, 'Did you kill Matthew Harper?' To which Timothy replied, 'Yes, I killed Matthew.'

The judge, annoyed that Timothy refused to answer any of the other questions put to him, was reluctant to let him off the stand. But after half an hour of resistance the judge could do little else. Timothy was dismissed and the jury adjourned to reach their verdict.

The verdict reached in the hall outside the court-room was clear. Those who came to offer their support felt cheated and tears trickled down their betrayed faces. In the end it was them who were in need of support. Timothy was fine. He had accepted his fate a long time ago. After all, he was guilty.

When he re-entered the court, the spectators' emotions were causing havoc. They seemed more nervous than he was. The jury took their seats and the whole court was instructed to stand for the judge. It seemed like everyone in the courtroom was waiting to be sentenced, as this case did not only involve the fate of Timothy Weston, but the fate of humanity itself. The actions of one reflect on all.

'Has the jury reached its decision?' echoed the voice of the very tired, resigned judge.

'We have, your Honour.'

'What say you?'

Silence.

'In the case of the murder of Matthew Harper we find the defendant, Timothy Weston, guilty.'

It would be wrong to say that this verdict was surprising. There was no other conclusion that could have been reached when the defendant was so adamant about his own guilt, but that did not decrease the sense of shock and loss felt by all. Those that were present in the court and the millions of others that were watching it on the news, in the comfort of their own living rooms felt the loss. It felt like, in that second, childhood and innocence were lost by humanity, to the point of no return.

The judge sighed. He wasn't surprised either, but he was not willing to condemn an eleven-year-old boy to ten years' imprisonment, no matter what the crime. He requested that Timothy come before him and then asked again the question that Timothy had been hounded with over the last few months, that he had never answered.

'Timothy, you've heard the decision,' he said

gravely. 'Before I sentence you, however, I'd like you to answer one question for me: What exactly did you do?'

Timothy looked up. He had refused to answer this question for so long that he nearly declined out of habit. However, he felt that he owed something to society. He felt that he had let the world down to such an extent that he should give them something back. They had a right to know.

'I told him I wished he was dead,' he mumbled.

Silence.

He spoke louder. 'The last time I saw Matthew, we had an argument and I told him that I wished he was dead.'

I am Ruairidh

Helen Whittaker

I am Ruairidh

I am Ruairidh. My name means 'red' in Gaelic, and it suits me, for I am a fiery red all over. I am one of the horses that run free on the wild moors, tamed by the Celtic tribe of Dhòmhnuill for riding and harness.

Legally, I belonged to the chief, as he owned the land I lived upon. I came and went where I pleased, and was happy to be called upon occasionally by the Dhòmhnuill for labour.

All of that changed as the Roman men from the midday horizon came. At first, I only glimpsed them from afar. The soldiers were wearing thick red tunics and shiny body armour, and were armed heavily, as though they suspected attack any second. They seemed to mistrust any local being, man or horse. One day, with Alasdair, eldest son of the chief and my master, on my back, I cantered past a troop of them. I could see the leader eyeing me, impressed. I thought nothing more of it, until one night after I had been harnessed for ploughing a patch of land. Alasdair had simply removed my bridle, rubbed my shoulder affectionately, then turned and walked off into the gloom.

I called once after him, then set off to find my own kindred, to gallop across the hills and eat the lush grass that grew in the glens. As I turned my head to the wind, I caught a strange scent. Men. A sweaty, foreign kind of man. Instinctive alarms warned me to get away. I wheeled, about to run to the safety of the village, but it was too late. A loop of thick rope had whistled through the air, and I was caught by the neck. The noose began to draw tight as I backed up in panic. I saw a flash of shiny armour, and a short, simple, ugly sword, nothing like the elegantly crafted weapons of the local smiths. Horse thieves! Romans!

I reared up on to my hind legs, bracing my body against the pull of the thick rope, and a sharp cracking sound rang out. I felt burning pain sear across my shoulder – the result of a long, leather whip. It was a new, painful and humiliating experience.

I fought the rope for a few minutes, then I realised that I was struggling against an immovable object. The Romans had tied the other end of the rope to a tree stump, and stood, just out of hoof reach, laughing coldly as my energy waned.

As I became still, but by no means submissive, one spoke. 'Now, brute,' he growled (horses can understand all languages, but the tongue he spoke was harsh to my ears), 'you'd better not resist if you know what's good for you.' As he spoke I heard a click and a crackle. He had lit a branch, and within a minute each of his comrades had a flaming torch. My ears flattened against my head. All horses fear fire.

The speaker went and untied the other end of the rope. They dragged me away from the only world I had known, to a dark, extensive building rising like a squat, ugly mountain out of the night.

This was a Roman fort, and it housed more men than I had ever seen, all alike with black hair and arrogant features. With the whip cracking behind me I stepped warily into a dark, rank-smelling, enclosed area. The closest thing I could think of to compare it to was a cave, but this was not like any cave I'd ever seen before. This was a stable, the gaol of all imprisoned horses.

Yet another Roman, who seemed to be in charge of the stables, removed the rope around my neck with one swift twist of his knife. He slammed the door on me before I could make my bid for freedom, and I was left alone.

Hungry and thirsty, I bent my head to the floor, and discovered that it was stone. I systematically kicked at every single bit of the walls and door, hoping desperately that I could batter them down and run home, to the heathery hills and green glens, and call for help. When I had accomplished nothing but a sore knee to add to my troubles, I moved over to the corner furthest from the door, and dozed uneasily.

After what seemed like endless hours in the dark, foul prison, I heard heavy footsteps on the stones outside. The door to my stable crashed open. Sunlight streamed in. I sprang out, ready to run home, but the man in charge of the stables blocked my way, a whip in one hand, and a long, slender stick in the other.

'Back, you unruly beast!' I remembered the cuts from such instruments used during my capture, and stepped back fearfully, my ears laid flat against my head in mistrust. Over his shoulder was slung a complicated-looking bridle, and he, with quick skill, placed the reins over my head, and planted his hand firmly on me. I flung my head up, and jumped as the long stick cut into my side. After that I held my head low enough, and he pushed a thick, cold bit into my mouth, and attached a chain round my chin. He then buckled up the numerous straps. I hated the bridle, and longed for the simple native style: a slender, light bit and a piece of leather leading from that, around behind the ears and down again, and then the reins.

'Well, my barbarian horse, I, Stablemaster Magnus Flavius, am your master now, and you will become a cavalry horse for a worthy cause, not for the painted savages,' he said, and left, only to return a second later with a strange, new harness: a saddle. The Dhòmhnuill had never bothered with such things, for there is a strong understanding between them and their animals.

The saddle was heavy and uncomfortable, and the girth that held it tight pinched my skin. As Magnus Flavius led me out, with a sharp tug against my mouth, I looked around to see my whereabouts in daylight. I was entirely enclosed within a courtyard, and Romans came and went freely, for this was a Roman barracks. With difficulty, Stablemaster Magnus hauled himself up into the saddle. Although he was not nearly as tall as the men of Dhòmhnuill were, he was heavier, and strained my back. He jabbed sharp spur shanks into my sides, and I sprang forward, snorting in surprise. He wrenched my head round, and we struggled for a minute. Eventually, he poked my sides again, and I understood this time. I decided to move forward at a speed that suited the obstinate man.

He rode me slowly round the courtyard, my hooves making the strangest clattering sound on the hard flagstones below. He used his whip and spurs often to correct me, and after one lap of the courtyard, we went out into a fenced-off field. He pushed his spurs in so sharply they drew blood. I reared up, and lunged, flinging my heels up, trying to rid myself of this demon on my back. He hung on grimly, punishing me with all of his strength. I bolted alongside the perimeter of the field, and this seemed to please him, for his spurs didn't touch my sides.

Days became weeks and weeks turned into

months, and I became used to this undignified style of being ridden, as though I were witless. But other shocks still came my way. One day I was led out in just a bridle, to smell burning skin and wood, and hot iron, similar to that which I used to smell near the forge in the village of the Dhòmhnuill, where the swords were made. I saw a Roman with a leather apron covering his soldier's tunic. He held a steaming piece of iron formed in a strange shape. Stablemaster Magnus tied me up, and stood near my head. The next instant, I felt a searing pain along my left flank. I squealed at the injustice of injuring a foe while he was tied up, but Stablemaster Magnus stroked my head, misinterpreting my squeal for one of pain. His touch made my skin crawl, and his hands had a sliminess no skin could feel, but could sense. I flinched and turned my head away, enraged by the betrayal. Out of the corner of my eye, I could see four accursed letters beginning to take form, blackened against my skin: SPQR.

This was not all, for as well as burning my flank with hot iron, scarring me permanently, the men attached metal to each of my hooves, so as my feet were heavy and I clattered noisily on the stone floor. I learned quickly, however, that the shoes on my feet made men fear my kick, and that I could have inflicted serious damage upon my captors, had I been the kind of horse to take advantage of such a situation.

Whilst I had lived freely and gone where I pleased and eaten when I wanted to, I would never have taken advantage of any man or beast. But those days seemed like a distant dream, fading in the cold, bleak morning light, and I was becoming embittered by my long imprisonment. I had to eat disgusting grain, drink stagnant water, stand still for hour upon tedious hour alone in a dark stable, and the only relief, if it could be perceived as relief, was when a fool would come and attempt to master me with cruelty. Was it any wonder that my tortured, home-sick mind began to tempt me with ideas of revenge against my captors?

My education as a Roman cavalry horse contin-ued. After a while, I was permitted to join the cavalry troops, and spent my days doing tedious drills that strained my muscles, because the lumpish Stable-master Magnus was always riding me. Nonetheless, I enjoyed pivoting on my hind legs, rearing and leaping as I had done with Alasdair on my back. It was the first sign of hope, and for a spell I forgot my ideas of revenge. I willingly accepted the cold bit and heavy saddle, despite my foolish handler and his wicked spurs and whip, his deliberate jerks that jabbed excruciatingly at my mouth.

One day, as the autumnal rain drizzled constantly, making a fine mist, which shrouded all objects and obscured all vision, the stupidity of my handler climaxed. His hands were heavier than usual, making the repetitive drills unbearable. I made one mistake, because he gave me the wrong signal, and the dreaded whip smacked my side and the bit tore into my tender mouth. A torrent of emotions that had been pent up since my capture flooded forth, and furiously I bucked, and the foam from my lips ran red. Suddenly, with curious satisfaction on my part, Magnus tumbled off my back and down to the flag-stones. The pain in my mouth was agonising, and I could not resist. He heaved himself up, and cut into me sharply again. I kicked, upsetting another cavalry horse, which reared, screaming. The poor beast fell over backwards on top of his rider and crushed him there on the cold stone floor. The drill practice was dismissed hurriedly and a medic summoned, to no avail. The man was dead, and I felt no sympathy and no remorse.

I went over and over the event in my mind whilst in my pitch black stable that night. I had been pushed too far, and was ready to retaliate. Thoughts of freedom and revenge gnawed away at my mind.

The opportunity came less than two weeks later. I was awoken from my slumber by Magnus, who looked flustered and carried a flaming torch. He placed the torch in a bracket, and flung on my saddle and bridle. 'The time has come, horse,' he said.

'Now is the time to prove yourself as a true Roman cavalry horse. The barbarians mean war, and we must secure our lands and drive them out if possible.' He paused and sighed. 'I fear that we shall pass to the Elysian Fields before sunrise. I wish . . .' and he trailed off, staring at a fixed point on the wall. He shook his head, and led me out.

It was dark outside, and the rest of the cavalry troop was already waiting. There was a sense of uneasiness, in both horses and men. Infantry soldiers, carrying large rectangular shields, marched past with the air of men going to their doom.

Magnus hauled himself up and into the saddle, and dug his spurs into me. As one, the cavalry troop cantered out into the night.

We pounded over the dark ground, heading to a specific point, from which attack against my people would be launched. Magnus ordered the halt, and we stood atop a hill, looking down on a glen, waiting. We were silent, save for the gentle champing of bits and stamping of hooves. The time had come.

With a neigh of fury, I spun round, my hooves flying in all directions. Magnus fell heavily on to my neck, unbalanced, and I continued, whirling like a devil, making the foolish, highly-strung Roman horses afraid and panicky. They were so easy to manipulate.

Chaos reigned supreme. Most of the other horses

151

had bolted or thrown their riders, and I had to do likewise to win my freedom. I bucked, as I never had before, using tricks I had used as a light-footed and light-hearted foal, corkscrewing, jack-knifing, rearing, and twisting. At long last, the parasite upon my back flew off. He hit the ground with a thud, and his head cracked against a rock. He lay still, dead, and the entire world would think that he had died in war, not at my hooves. I hoped that the last thought in his cruel mind was that he was being paid for his role in my torture.

At once I raced away, instinct leading me to my beloved Dhòmhnuill. As I ran, I realised my sides were streaked with blood, and my mouth ached from my battle. Out of the dark, came shapes I had thought I would never see again, tall, blond men. Natives. I came forward, and saw that they were not the Dhòmhnuill at all! They were Chaluim, who lived half a day's ride from the Dhòmhnuill village. Nonetheless, they were allies.

One of them removed my bridle and saddle, and led me to a stream. He bathed my sides in the cool cleansing water, and I drank, feeling, for the first time in many months, like I was truly thought of as an assistant and loyal beast, no longer a slave.

I heard a voice behind me. 'That was some impressive work, Ruairidh, stampeding the cavalry. I thought I would never see you again.'

I turned, and there stood Alasdair! I walked towards him, not sure if I was dreaming or not, and then rested my head on his broad shoulder. He rubbed his hand roughly on my forehead. The Chaluim who had brought me to the water said, 'He's yours, is he, Alasdair MacDhòmhnuill?' and Alasdair nodded.

'Yes, Fearchar MacChaluim, this is my steed, stolen by the Romans, and returned of his own free will.'

Alasdair gently placed a bridle over my head, a clean, simple bridle, the kind I had longed for during my emprisonment. He lifted himself up, and sat lightly on my back.

'Come, Ruairidh, we have work to do,' he said, and touched my sides delicately with his bare feet.

I was to join the cavalry of the native forces, who had combined in an attempt to drive out the Romans in one swoop.

With Alasdair on my back, I willingly faced the mighty Roman army spread out before us in the dark hour before dawn. The archers to my left fired upon the Roman infantry, and they used their massive shields to protect themselves, making a shape like a giant beetle, foul and dangerous.

Alasdair drew his slender sword and cried his war-cry aloud: 'Creagan an Fhithich! The Raven's Rock!' We advanced, others taking up the chant. We were very close to the beetle-like formation, and it began to break up as we crashed into it. The world we knew disintegrated into a frenzied slaughter. Alasdair was swinging his sword right, left and centre, and I did my own bit too, kicking Romans with my Roman-shod heels, and pivoting to assist Alasdair in the elimination of enemies. It appeared to me that the Celts were coming out on top, pushing back the Roman defence, and I could move freely. I reared, proud and defiant, and Alasdair cheered, raising his sword. Then a burning pain struck my chest.

I pitched forward on to four legs, seeing a black arrow sticking out from just below my neck. A Roman archer stood less than ten feet from me, holding a bow. I raced to meet him, feeling Alasdair trembling with rage. The archer stooped and picked up an axe. Alasdair parried the axe as it swung up at him, then in one fatal stroke, the archer swung it into my chest, and I shrieked as it came out again. I fell, my world going black, although the sun was rising and flooding the battlefield in gold. I heard Alasdair shout, having jumped clear, and the Roman fell headless beside me.

I could see nothing, but felt Alasdair's gentle hand resting on my neck, as life ebbed away with the flow of blood. With the enlightenment of one who is facing his death, I understood that all crimes bring punishment . . . life for a life. There can be no perfect crime.

Also available from Piccadilly Press, by
KERRY PARNELL

Street Smart is about safety. With practical guidelines, tips for common sense and advice on how to handle difficult situations with confidence, it can help you live your life safely and independently. The message is *be aware*, rather than *beware!* Kerry Parnell covers the issues teenagers face, such as:

- drugs and alcohol;
- dating and sex;
- safety on the street and on public transport;
- peer pressure and bullying;
- streetwise know-how – cash machines, pick-pockets, strangers;
- internet, email and phone savvy;
- avoiding or coping with abuse, harassment or assault;
- dealing with crime;
- and much more.

By the author of *Bliss - The Smart Girl's Guide to Sex*:
"This accessible and straightforward book . . . provides facts, reassurance and invaluable advice." *Publishing News*

Also available from Piccadilly Press, by
LOUISE RENNISON

Sunday 8.00 p.m.

Walking home, I said, "I don't think he's that keen on her. What sort of kiss do you think it was? Was there actual lip contact? Or was it lip to cheek, or lip to corner of mouth?"

"I think it was lip to corner of mouth, but maybe it was lip to cheek?"

"It wasn't **full-frontal snogging** though, was it?"

"No."

"I think she went for full-frontal and he converted it into lip to corner of mouth . . ."

Saturday 6.58 p.m.

Lindsay was wearing a thong! I don't understand **thongs** – what is the point of them? They just go up your bum, as far as I can tell!

Wednesday 10.30 p.m.

Mrs Next Door complained that **Angus** has been frightening their poodle again. He stalks it. I explained, "Well, he's a Scottish wildcat, that's what they do. They stalk their prey. I have tried to train him but he ate his lead."

"This is very funny – very, very funny. I wish I had read this when I was a teenager, it really is very funny." *Alan Davies*

'Joseph, are you in there? It's me, your mother.'

Damn, I thought it might be that Jennifer Lopez again; she usually calls round about this time for a quick snog.

- **ZULUS** I always think my life's a bit like living in that old film *Zulu* – you know, the one where Michael Caine (me) and a bunch of rather hot British soldiers (Rover) are holding this garrison fort in Africa somewhere against thousands of ever-so-cross natives (my family).

- **GIRLS** This is really sad. One minute my head's full of the gorgeous, sexy Jade, and whether I might stand a chance with her after all, and the next, I'm thinking of dear sweet Lucy. Jade–Lucy, Lucy–Jade, I just can't get my brain straight.

- **VIDEOS** I'm a complete cinema junkie – a filmoholic – a movie maniac – a video voyeur, you name it. I don't know why, but all I ever think about is films (oh yes – and girls).

"Lively, witty text by a diverting writer." *Publishing News*

In the same series: *Merlin, Movies and Lucy Something*
Sequins, Stardom and Chloe's Dad

Students have more than ever to learn at school these days, and there seems to be an endless succession of exams and assessments. This book aims to help you not only to master the skills of concentration, but also to relax. It may even help you to enjoy your studies!

Learn how to:

- get organised, work to a routine, yet be flexible and adaptable;
- work in your preferred learning style and with the eight forms of intelligence;
- recognise and overcome the limits you put on yourself;
- avoid the effects of dehydration, lack of oxygen and caffeine sensitivity;
- get into 'The Flow';
- and much, much more.

By the author of *Smart Thinking*:
"It's an engaging, clear and positive exploration of the nature of self-belief. Well worth making available – and reading yourself." *The Guardian*

If you would like more information about
books available from Piccadilly Press and how
to order them, please contact us at:

Piccadilly Press Ltd.
5 Castle Road
London
NW1 8PR

Tel: 020 7267 4492
Fax: 020 7267 4493

Feel free to visit our website at
www.piccadillypress.co.uk